"Listen, Pete," Stacy said, carefully avoiding his eyes, "I'm going to be really busy in the next few weeks. My father's going to be visiting for a few days, and he's getting here tomorrow. Also, we're having elections in my sorority, and I'm going to be pretty involved with the campaign."

"So? How's that going to change anything? I know you want to see your father, so the game's out. But we can still eat breakfast together, can't we?" He grinned. "Come on, I'll walk you to class."

Stacy hesitated, trying to ignore the way her heart was pounding. "I doubt I'll have time for breakfast. I've got a lot of campaigning to do. Plus I'm still behind with my midterm work, and . . ."

Stacy stole a look at him: his usual easy grin had faded and his jaw was clenched. He turned to confront her, his eyes intense. "I guess you're trying to tell me something," he said.

Stacy nodded. Funny. There was a time when she would have enjoyed being mean to him. But now she felt an unexpected wrenching deep inside her as she read the hurt in his eyes, and she had to look away.

Other books in the ROOMMATES series:

Roommates

CRASH COURSE
Susan Blake

BANTAM BOOKS
TORONTO • NEW YORK • LONDON • SYDNEY • AUCKLAND

CRASH COURSE

A BANTAM BOOK   0 553 17572 6

First publication in Great Britain

PRINTING HISTORY
Bantam edition published 1988

Bantam Books are published by Transworld Publishers Ltd.,
61–63 Uxbridge Road, Ealing, London W5 5SA,
in Australia by Transworld Publishers (Australia) Pty. Ltd.,
15–23 Helles Avenue, Moorebank, NSW 2170, and in New
Zealand by Transworld Publishers (N.Z.) Ltd., Cnr. Moselle
and Waipareira Avenues, Henderson, Auckland.

Printed and bound in Great Britain by
Hazell Watson & Viney Limited
Member of BPCC plc
Aylesbury, Bucks, England

CRASH COURSE

Chapter 1

Stacy Swanson held the magazine closer and studied the photo of the pencil-thin model in the cranberry cashmere sweater. Yes, it was exactly what she wanted. She had lost another pound this week, and the sweater's clingy silhouette would show off her slender figure. That color would be perfect with her blond hair, too. She picked up a pencil and began to sketch idly on the edge of the page. With a black belt draped at the hip and maybe a straight black skirt, the outfit would be just right for a dinner out in Boston when she went home for Thanksgiving.

She smiled at the sketch. Oh, it would be great to go back to Boston, to escape from this provincial little college stuck in the middle of nowhere. That was what she needed—to get back to civilization, where she could go to the theater if she felt like it or to an art show. Hawthorne College might be okay for some people, but not for somebody as sophisticated as Stacy Swanson.

All of a sudden, Stacy's suitemate Terry Conklin burst into suite 2C, waving an envelope. "I got it! I got it!" she cried excitedly. "Did you guys get yours?"

"Get my what?" asked Samantha Hill, coming out of the bedroom she and Stacy shared. Sam was wearing her usual preppy outfit—khaki cords, a turtleneck, and a black sweater. With her long, wheat-colored hair pulled into a ponytail, she looked like the all-American girl.

Terry flopped down on the sofa next to Stacy. "Why, your midterm grade report, that's what," she said. She pulled off her blue cardigan and tucked her white blouse into her gray skirt. Terry's outfits always reminded Stacy of the uniforms she'd worn in Swiss boarding school the year she'd been sent off to Europe while her mother was getting her second divorce. They were certainly not something *she'd* wear by choice.

Terry looked at Stacy. "How'd you do, Stacy? What did you get?"

Stacy turned the page. "Why do you want to know?" she asked nonchalantly.

Stacy *had* gotten her grade report, but she hadn't opened it. At least she assumed that was what she'd gotten in the mail this morning, along with a note from Sydney, her mother, inviting her to spend Thanksgiving Day with Sydney and her friend David in Vermont. The ski resort where they'd be staying would probably be crawling with guys from

Cornell and Williams . . . maybe she'd meet somebody really exciting. At any rate, someone more exciting than the guys at Hawthorne—but then, it wouldn't take much for that to happen, Stacy thought.

"Terry's asking about *your* grades because she wants to tell us about *hers*," Roni Davies remarked. Roni, who shared the other bedroom in the suite with Terry, was sitting on the floor, pulling curlers out of her frizzy auburn hair and listening to a record. She was dressed in one of her more conservative outfits: a pair of black leotards and a bright orange jungle-print silk T-shirt. From head to toe, Roni wasn't what you'd expect of a southern debutante.

"Okay," Stacy said with a sigh, turning to Terry. "Tell us how you did on your midterms." Really. Terry was *such* a grade-grubber sometimes, Stacy thought.

Roni dropped her comb and began to snap her fingers and dance to the music. "Yeah, come on, Terry," she said. "What's your payoff for all that bookworming? Do you get a free pass to medical school?"

Terry made a face at Roni. "Well, if you really want to know," she said, propping her feet on the coffee table and taking off her tortoiseshell-rimmed glasses, "I did okay."

"That means you aced everything." Roni stood up and went to the compact refrigerator in the corner. "Right?" She took out a diet soda and a half-empty jar of pickles.

Terry put her glasses back on. "Well, I didn't exactly get *all* A's," she confessed. She smiled. "But I *am* pulling an A in organic."

Sam glanced admiringly at Terry. "Wow, Terry," she said, "I'm really impressed. I don't think I know anybody else who could get an A in organic chemistry. In fact, I didn't even know it was *possible* to get an A in organic. How'd you do in the rest of your courses?" That was Sam for you, Stacy thought, always interested in other people. It was the thing she admired most about Sam.

"I'm getting a B in biology," said Terry. She pulled out her grade report. "But I think I can bring that up to an A before finals. And I got an A in English and an A in psych." She looked at Roni. "So how'd you do?"

Roni turned off the stereo and sat back down on the floor, soda in one hand, jar of pickles in the other. "Nothing to write home about," she admitted. "B's and C's. I got a C in English because I got an Incomplete on the last paper. But Richards gave me a B in ecology, which I wasn't expecting, so I got off okay." She fished a pickle out of the jar with a ballpoint pen and put it in her mouth. "I'll bet you aced everything, huh, Sam?"

Sam's ponytail bobbed as she shook her head. "Don't I wish. But Dr. Lewis gave me an A in political science."

"Well, he *ought* to," Stacy added, "after the way that demonstration turned out." She opened the magazine to her sketch and picked up her pencil again. Maybe a hat, a fedora, would complete the outfit. "I mean, you were lucky you didn't get suspended."

Sam blushed. "Let's not talk about that. I'm just glad the whole thing's over."

Stacy couldn't blame Sam for not wanting to talk about it. Sam and a group of other students had staged a campus demonstration for a political science project, but the leader of the group had gotten carried away with the protest and had attracted a large crowd. When the crowd had started to chant, campus security had showed up to arrest the demonstrators—including Sam.

Stacy added a feather to the hat she'd just sketched. The whole thing with Sam had been kind of odd, actually. Samantha Hill wasn't exactly the type of girl you'd expect to get involved in radical politics. It must have been the influence of her political science professor, or maybe Aaron Goldberg.

At the thought of Aaron, Stacy's stomach muscles knotted with jealousy. She pushed him out of her mind. It wasn't a good idea for her to think about Aaron and Sam or the fact that *she* had liked him first. Anyway, there were plenty of guys in her life —like Mark, the boy she'd gone out with Friday night, or that Beta brother who'd called her again tonight, or Alex, the guy she'd danced with at the Alpha Pi party last week. Alex was a terrific dancer, and she'd had a great time flirting with him. He was clever and witty, even if he *was* sort of arrogant. But it was hard not to think about Aaron. It wasn't just that she happened to like him. She hated being upstaged—especially by her own roommate. Things like that *never* happened to Stacy.

"So what about you, Stacy?" Terry was asking. "How'd you do in your classes?"

Stacy gave a careless shrug. "I don't know," she said, admiring the outfit she'd sketched. "I haven't opened my 'report card.'"

"You haven't opened it?" Terry asked, disbelieving. "How can you stand the suspense?"

Stacy put down her pencil and looked at Terry. "Because grades aren't such a big deal to me," she said. That wasn't exactly true. Getting good grades had seemed important, at least back in prep school. But she was beginning to feel bored with this whole discussion. "Anyway, it's only midterms." She stretched and yawned. "Who worries about a C or two at midterms?"

"Well, if you feel that way about it . . ." Roni picked up Stacy's calfskin bag, sitting on the table at the end of the sofa. The grade report envelope was sticking out of the top. "Here it is," said Roni, pulling out the envelope. "Let's see how you did."

Alarmed, Stacy reached for the envelope. "Hey," she said, "that's *mine*. You don't have any right to—"

But Roni had already ripped open the envelope with a dramatic flourish, as if she were giving out an Oscar, and now she began to read aloud in a big, important voice: "Miss Anastasia Vaughn Swanson, suite two C, Rogers House. Art 101, F. Music 105, F." Her eyes widened suddenly, and her voice slowed. "English 102, D. Art 106—" She gulped. "Art 106, F."

"Oh, come on, Roni," Terry said in an exasperated voice. "Stop fooling around. *Nobody* fails Music Appreciation—it's a Mickey Mouse course. And with Stacy's talent for drawing, there's no way she could flunk art." She grabbed the report out of Roni's hand. Then she stared up at Stacy, her brown eyes huge and unbelieving.

"God, Stacy, I can't believe this," she whispered.

"Give me that," Stacy said between clenched teeth. She snatched the report from Terry's frozen hands. Without looking at it, she crumpled it into a tiny ball and stood up, the palms of her hands clammy. "I hope you've had your fun," she said to Roni, in an icily controlled voice. She turned and glared at Terry and Sam. "I hope you've *all* enjoyed this little game."

"I'm sorry, Stacy, really I am," Roni said. "Please don't . . . " She stood up and tried to put her arm around Stacy's shoulder, but Stacy angrily brushed her away.

"We didn't mean any harm, Stacy," Terry said, looking as if she were going to burst into tears. "I'm really sorry, honest. I wish there was something I could—"

"Maybe there's some sort of mistake," Sam said hopefully. "Maybe the computer screwed up, or—"

"No, it's no mistake," Stacy said, the anger draining away, leaving her weak and empty. She felt tired, so tired she could hardly stand up. "I really *did* bomb everything. I knew this was going to happen." She looked at her suitemates, who were watching her carefully. There was such concern in their eyes that suddenly Stacy felt a little overwhelmed by their kindness.

"I'm sorry for blowing up," she said. "It's just that. . ." She swallowed. "It's just that. . ." She blinked to keep the tears from coming. "Listen, you guys, I don't think I want to talk right now. I'm really tired. I . . . I'm going to lie down for a little while."

The phone rang, and Roni went to answer it while Terry put her arm around Stacy's shoulders. "Are you sure you don't want to talk?" she asked worriedly. "You shouldn't keep all your emotions bottled up. You should let your feelings out. Can't we talk?"

Roni looked up from the phone. "It's for Stacy. Somebody named Alex."

"I don't want to talk to Alex right now," Stacy said. She knew she wouldn't be coherent.

Sam opened the door to their bedroom. "I think a nap is exactly what you need. I'll get a blanket."

Stacy followed Sam into the bedroom. Maybe she'd be able to cope with the fact that she was actually *failing* her first semester of college if she only got enough sleep for once.

Stacy felt as though she'd been asleep for only a few minutes, but it was already dark outside when she heard a gentle knock on the door.

"Stacy, it's nearly six, and we're all going over to the PizzaRoo. Want to come with us?"

Stacy buried her head under the pillow, but she could still hear Terry's voice.

"Hey, Stace, come on." Terry rattled the knob a

little. "You'll feel better after you've had something to eat."

Stacy shuddered and rolled over on her side, pulling her knees up to her chest. The *last* thing she needed was pizza loaded with cheese and sausage. Ugh. Just the thought of all those hundreds of calories made her feel fat.

"Oh, leave her alone, why don't you?" It was Roni's voice. "Anyway, she's probably still asleep."

"But she's going to make herself sick if she doesn't start eating better. Have you noticed how skinny she is?" Terry paused. "Maybe she's anorexic."

Anorexic? Stacy yanked the pillow down harder, covering her ears. Where did Terry get such a ridiculous idea? Sure, she wanted to lose weight, but she wasn't anorexic. And she wasn't skinny, either—she was *slim*.

"Listen, if Stacy's not going with us, we ought to get started. I told Aaron I'd go running with him at seven-thirty." As usual, Sam was being reasonable.

"I'm just worried about her, that's all," Terry muttered. Her voice faded a little, as if she'd stepped away from the door. "Did you see her face when she looked at that grade report?" Stacy sat up and pushed the pillow away, straining to hear what Terry was saying. "It was like she'd been hit. She got absolutely white, with a sort of blank look, like shock. Actual trauma, the kind my psych teacher was talking about."

"Terry," Roni inquired, "has anybody warned you lately about practicing psychology without a license?

That wasn't trauma, it was plain old surprise. You'd be surprised too, if you'd just learned that you were flunking out. But then, you'd never do that."

There was another pause, and then Sam said, "I guess it was pretty rude—reading her grade report out loud, I mean. I wouldn't have wanted somebody to do that to me."

"Well, I certainly wouldn't have done it if I'd known it was going to turn out like this," Roni said in a defensive tone. "You just never know how Stacy's going to react. Sometimes she's really up, and she doesn't mind teasing. Other times the slightest thing ticks her off."

Stacy shifted uncomfortably, wishing she couldn't hear what they were saying—but at the same time she was too curious *not* to listen. She was beginning to get very angry about what she heard.

"It's been getting worse in the last couple of weeks, too," Roni went on. "She's started doing weird things, things that don't fit her. She's always been so classy—with those superexpensive clothes and that new Mercedes and that sophisticated Boston accent. All the girls on the floor envy her. They'd love to trade places with her."

"Why wouldn't they?" asked Terry. "She's got everything people dream about—money to burn, sophistication, good looks."

Stacy smiled to herself. It was true. Everybody envied her—and she loved it.

"Yeah," Roni said, "that's just my point. She's got everything, but then she starts doing crazy things.

Like last week, when she got her hair cut punk and dyed pink and lavender. I mean, I like punk, but it just isn't Stacy's thing. And now, here she is, a very intelligent girl flunking out." Roni paused. "What do you think, Sam? You're her roommate. You know her better than we do."

"I'm not sure I know her any better," Sam replied, thinking. "She's hard to get close to. But you're right, getting her hair dyed like that *was* pretty strange. And she seemed to be sorry as soon as she'd done it. She *has* been cutting class a lot. I guess that's why . . ."

Stacy put her hands over her ears, the anger burning a hole in her stomach. Weren't these people supposed to be her friends? Here they were, making judgments about her, talking like they had her psychoanalyzed, when they didn't know the first thing about her! She wished they'd stop talking and leave —but she couldn't resist listening. She pulled her hands away.

"That's why she flunked everything," Terry said, finishing Sam's sentence. "Listen, don't you think it would be a good idea to talk to her? Or maybe we should talk to our RA or something. I mean, really try to help her get on the right track—"

"Hey, you guys," Roni interrupted, "can't we worry about Stacy over a pizza?" The closet door slammed. "Has anybody seen my sweatshirt? I could swear I left it right here, hanging on the back of the—"

"It's on the sofa," Terry told her.

"Oh, yeah." Stacy heard Roni's laugh, slightly muffled, as if she were pulling her sweatshirt over her head. "Well, come on. If we're going, let's go."

As the door to the suite closed, Stacy threw the pillow at the wall as hard as she could.

Chapter 2

Feeling a little better after her nap, Stacy sat cross-legged on her bed, her back against the wall. She stroked the long white ears of her stuffed rabbit. "You wouldn't talk about me behind my back, would you, Reggie?" she whispered. "And it doesn't matter to you whether I get an A or an F—you still love me anyway, don't you?" She wasn't angry anymore, just hurt. If her suitemates really cared about her, they wouldn't talk about her that way. They shouldn't make judgments. Anyway, what had she done that was so awful? Was dyeing your hair a crime? She'd only cut a few classes, had a problem or two with her courses. It wasn't anything she couldn't fix, if she put her mind to it. She'd been in worse situations before.

She rested her cheek against Reggie's warm, comforting fur. "It's going to be all right," she said.

After a minute, she put the bunny down, went

13

into the bathroom, and turned on the hot water. A good shower always cleared her head, no matter what was bothering her. What did people do to relax before showers were invented? she wondered.

As she took off her clothes, Stacy caught sight of herself in the mirror and frowned. She still had a little bulge around the waist. In spite of the fact that she'd gotten down to 113, she really needed to lose more. She was fairly tall—five feet seven—and the charts said that her ideal weight was about 125. But when she weighed 125 she felt like the Goodyear blimp, and her clothes looked terrible on her. If she could manage to get down to 110, she'd have the perfect body.

Stacy stretched her arms over her head, admiring her slender thighs, her flat—well, almost flat—stomach, delicate wristbones. Still, there was that bulge to get rid of. She'd have to run more and eat less for a while. She was only running four miles a day now—she could easily go to four and a half or five. She had been fasting only one day a week, why not make it two *consecutive* days? With all that extra effort, and a few diet pills, she'd be down to 110 before Thanksgiving. She'd be in fabulous shape for the holiday parties—and for that cashmere sweater she wanted to get.

Stacy stepped under the steaming spray, opened the shampoo, and began to wash her hair. Already she felt more energetic. Bad as her grades might seem, improving them was only a matter of doing some minor catch-up work. If that didn't do it, she would talk to her professors and convince them that she'd had a few adjustment problems. It could happen to anybody in their freshman year. And if *that* didn't work—well, she could always transfer to another college. It wasn't as if she were *stuck* at Hawthorne—she could go anywhere she wanted. She smiled confidently. Yes, everything was going to be fine. She'd been in sticky situations before, and she'd always managed to pull them off.

Stacy tilted her face up and let the hot water run through her short hair. She was glad that she'd gotten it cut the week before. Of course, Roni was right—it was stupid to dye it those ridiculous colors. She could hardly remember *why* she'd done it, except that sometimes she had this overwhelming desire to change *everything* about herself. But now that the natural blond color was back, she liked having her hair short. It looked elegant, she thought, the way it was cut close to her head and spiked into sideburns at her cheekbones. In fact, it was just perfect for her new slender image.

Twenty minutes later, Stacy had put on her burgundy robe and was taking a fresh bottle of mineral water and a lime out of the refrigerator. She had everything she needed to study—except her art history textbook. She was behind in her reading assignment by a couple of chapters, but it was easy stuff. If she started now, she'd be caught up by bedtime.

Stacy found her book lying behind a pillow in the corner of the sofa, so she sat down and prepared herself to be bored. A few minutes later, she was already daydreaming and looking around the room for some distraction to save her.

The suite wasn't exactly a model of interior decorating, even though Rogers House was the oldest dorm on campus, and suite 2C had large rooms with wooden floors and high ceilings. Sam and Terry had put some potted plants on the balcony, and the living room walls were covered with posters and art prints —most of which Stacy had put up. Roni's contribution, a neon beer sign, blinked gaudily in one corner. Stacy tried not to look at it. If you disregarded the sign, the room looked, Stacy thought, a little like the light and airy Paris *pension* where she'd stayed when she'd escaped from her mother's plush hotel for a few days last summer.

Stacy forced her attention back to her book. If she were going to study, she'd better get started. But she had just started to read when the telephone rang. Maybe it's Alex calling again, she thought. She marked her place in the chapter and picked up the phone.

"Hello, Stacy, it's Sydney."

Ever since Stacy could remember, her mother had insisted on being called Sydney. She had to admit that the name fit her mother very well—much better than "Mother" or "Mom." Sydney was beautiful, elegant, aristocratic—she was from an old, elite Boston family—and very nearly perfect. She was almost *too* perfect.

Stacy sighed. "Hi, Sydney, how are things in Boston? How's everything at the gallery?" Sydney owned an exclusive art gallery just off the Commons, on Beacon Hill. She and Stacy lived near the gallery, in a townhouse filled with valuable art and antiques from Boston's early days. That is, Sydney lived there when she wasn't rushing off to some exotic place after a collector's item or flying to her condo on Maui.

"That's not the question, is it, my dear? The question is, how are *you*, and what in the world is going on at that college of yours?"

Stacy swallowed. "I'm not sure I understand the question. Nothing's going on here. Right now I'm doing my art history homework."

"Stacy, love, please don't play games with me." Sydney paused. "I have your grade report."

"Oh." Why hadn't it occurred to her that Hawthorne might send her grades to her mother? "Well, I—"

"What are you doing down there at Hawthorne?" Sydney demanded crossly. "Since you absolutely insisted on going there, I'd think that you'd at least make a minimal effort to do well. At Vassar, I'm sure you would have..."

Blah, blah, blah. Stacy picked up a pencil and began to sketch, tuning out her mother's voice. Sydney had expected her to attend Vassar, where Sydney and *her* mother had graduated—both senior class presidents, both summa cum laude. Stacy didn't have anything *against* Vassar, but she'd decided halfway through her senior year at Elizabeth Deere that she'd had enough of her mother's suggestions on what she should do with her life. Without telling Sydney, she'd talked to the counselor about other schools—

specifically *not* Vassar and *not* in the Northeast. Before Sydney knew anything about it, Stacy had been
accepted at Hawthorne, a small but very good college in Hawthorne Springs, Georgia, sixty miles
north of Atlanta. Of course, as Sydney had pointed
out in a horrified tone, Hawthorne Springs was absolutely *nowhere*. But that was exactly what Stacy
wanted—a college her mother hadn't chosen, in a
town where she wasn't likely to drop in for a visit.

When Sydney had found out that Stacy wasn't
going to Vassar, she'd thrown a temper tantrum, in
her own way. Not a huge explosion—that wasn't her
style. She'd simply refused to pay the housing deposit
or the tuition. But Stacy had gotten the money from
her father, and there was nothing Sydney could do
except tell Stacy what a hideous mistake she was
making.

That was exactly what she'd done, over and over,
and she was still doing it. ". . . so if you're not happy
at Hawthorne," Sydney was saying, "we can make
other arrangements. If you're set against Vassar,
there's always Brown or Williams. My friend
Spencer is on the board at Brown, and he'd be
glad—"

Stacy's fingers tightened nervously around her
pencil as she continued to sketch. "Thanks, Sydney,"
she said, carefully keeping her voice under control,
"but that's really not necessary. I *like* Hawthorne."
She took a deep breath. "I am extremely happy here.
I adore my suitemates, and I *love* my classes. I intend
to stay." So much for her idea about transferring—
now she'd really have to work hard.

"But I don't understand. If you love your classes, why are your grades so *abysmally* low?"

Just then Stacy glanced down at her sketch. She'd drawn a cartoon of a dragon, with fire flaring out of its nostrils. She smiled grimly: if Terry saw it, she'd probably find enough psychological significance to write her next paper about it. "Oh, it's just a combination of things," she said to Sydney in a casual voice. "I didn't finish my pottery project in art, and I'm behind a paper or two in English. No big deal. And I guess I missed a couple of quizzes in art history." All of which was true, although there was a little more to it than that.

"I don't understand about art," Sydney said. "With your talent, you ought to be getting an A. And music? You're actually failing music? My God, Stacy, I've spent a fortune on music lessons, and you've had season tickets to the symphony for years. How could you possibly—?"

"Look, Sydney," Stacy said, "it's only music appreciation. I'll be able to make it up." She put a smile into her voice. "Really, there's nothing to worry about. All the professors give low midterm grades. They do it to make you work harder." This was very probably true, Stacy reminded herself.

"You're *sure* you like it there?"

Stacy summoned all her enthusiasm. "It's wonderful," she said, making her voice bubble. "The sorority is *great*, I'm getting involved, and I have loads of friends."

"Well, I'm glad to hear about the sorority. It would be delightful if you'd run for office. I loved being president my senior year." She paused. "What about your weight, Stacy? Are you keeping your weight up?"

Stacy flinched. She couldn't imagine why, but her mother seemed to *want* her to look like a blimp. She was always trying to get Stacy to eat more.

"Oh, I'm working on it," she said evasively, and changed the subject. "Have you seen Jason?"

Jason was Stacy's father. He and Sydney had been divorced when Stacy was quite young. But Stacy visited him fairly often in his posh apartment in Boston's Copley Square.

"No, I haven't," Sydney said in a frosty tone. "I don't suppose you've heard from him."

"No," Stacy admitted. "But I'm sure I'll see him at Thanksgiving. He promised—"

"Oh, yes, that's something else we simply must talk about," Sydney broke in. "David and I may change our Thanksgiving plans. But I've just this instant realized what time it is. I'm sorry, dear, but David will be here any minute. I have to dash."

"Wait," Stacy said hurriedly, "what about Thanksgiving? Aren't we going to the lodge?"

"No time now, sweetheart," Sydney said. "I'm glad to hear that everything is going well, and we'll talk later about the holidays. Bye."

Stacy stared at the phone. A change of plans for Thanksgiving? Well, if they didn't go to Vermont, she'd have more time to spend with her father. He was running for office again this year—his fourth term as state senator—but the elections would be over by that time. No doubt he'd be feeling good about his victory, and they could have a terrific time together, just the two of them.

Stacy tried to read again, but after a few minutes she put her book down. Talking to Sydney invariably made her feel a little anxious, and very restless. She always felt as if she hadn't quite measured up to her mother's expectations. Well, it was only seven-thirty. She could read later. Right now she wanted to go jogging.

In the bedroom, Stacy changed into a pair of gold running shorts and pulled on her new sneakers. She fastened a pair of cuff weights around her wrists. Catching a glimpse of herself in the mirror, she sucked in her stomach. That bulge *really* had to go. Filled with determination, she headed for the door. But just as she was about to open it, there was a knock. Standing in the hallway, tall and handsome even in baggy gray sweatpants and a sweatshirt, was Aaron Goldberg. Stacy's heartbeat quickened.

"Hi, Stacy," Aaron said. "Is Sam around?"

"Uh, no, she isn't," Stacy replied. She steadied herself with a deep breath. Darn it. How could she be so attracted to a guy who'd rather date her roommate? She stepped out into the hallway beside him and closed the door.

"Oh?" Aaron lifted an eyebrow. "Where'd she go? Did she say when she'd be back?"

Stacy thought for a second. She wasn't supposed to know where her suitemates had gone or what time they'd be coming back. "I don't know," she finally said, shrugging. "Everybody's gone. I was taking a nap when they left."

Aaron looked disappointed, but he smiled kindly anyway. "Looks like you're on your way to run," he said.

Stacy nodded, remembering that Aaron and Sam had been going to run together. Sam ought to be more careful about the time, she thought. If *she'd* had a date with Aaron, she wouldn't be late. "Yeah," she said. "Want to run with me?"

Aaron glanced at his watch. "I'll jog once around the lake with you, then come back here. How's that?"

Stacy shrugged. "Okay, I guess."

"Well, come on, then," he said. Stacy followed him down the stairs, her heart beating loudly. She began to wonder if being close to Aaron would always have this effect on her.

The brisk evening breeze held a November chill, but Stacy warmed up quickly, jogging along the broad path that circled Hawthorne Lake. Aaron had stripped down to running shorts, leaving his sweatpants and shirt on the bench beside the lake. Running behind him, Stacy could see his shoulder muscles gleaming with perspiration. Wouldn't it be wonderful to have those strong arms around her, to know that he wanted her? And that's what would have happened if Sam hadn't gotten in the way. What Sam had done wasn't fair, really. Stacy was the one who had called Aaron and invited him to the party, after they'd had lunch together *twice* the week before. But Sam was the one who'd left the party

with him—rubbing it in her face as they left together
—and stayed out all night. From that night on,
Aaron had been wrapped around Sam's little finger.

The anger grew stronger, pulsing with her strides.
It was *doubly* unfair, because Sam already *had* a
boyfriend, Jon, away at school somewhere in the
Midwest. They weren't going steady now, but Stacy
knew that Sam was going to see him at Thanksgiving. Maybe she ought to just leak that little piece
of information to Aaron. But no, she wouldn't stoop
that low—she didn't have to, anyway. Before long,
Aaron was bound to get bored with Sam—and if he
didn't, he wasn't the kind of guy she thought he was.

The path broadened as it curved up a gentle hill
and around the south end of the lake. Aaron slowed
a little so that Stacy could catch up with him. "The
campus is pretty at night, isn't it?" he asked as Stacy
drew alongside.

Stacy looked around her. Everybody was always
raving about how terrific the campus was, with its
clumps of pine trees and the sheer limestone bluff that
rose up to the north of the lake. But it was much too
rural for her, and Hawthorne Springs, pretty as it
was, was impossibly provincial. There was no decent
place to shop, except for one or two halfway interesting boutiques on Grove Street. And there was only
one movie theater. Maybe it seemed wonderful and
exciting to Sam, who came from a small town in
Illinois, but if they'd been to Paris and London,
Hawthorne Springs was very definitely *nowhere*.

Still, the campus did have its good points.
Hawthorne Hall had a Gothic tower that reminded

Stacy of a German church, and the ivy that covered the old redbrick buildings gave the campus an English look. The lake was nice, too, especially at night; the lights from the bridge that crossed the lake to the Commons sparkled like a diamond bracelet.

"Yeah, it's okay," Stacy replied. "If you like that sort of thing."

"Just okay?" Aaron asked. He ducked under a low-hanging tree and slowed to a walk.

"Well, you've lived in the city," Stacy said. Aaron had told her he was from New York. "Don't you get a little bored here?"

"Bored with the rural life, you mean?" he asked. He grinned. "Yeah, well, Hawthorne Springs *is* sort of out in the boonies, I guess. PizzaRoo isn't exactly in the same category as Lutèce or the Four Seasons."

Stacy looked at him. "Yeah, I love going out to dinner in New York. Boston's nice, too, though. Have you ever been there?"

"My brother practices law there. I go up on holidays."

"Thanksgiving?" she asked. A voice inside her said, *Hey, wait, why are you asking him this?* And another voice retorted, *Who cares?* She ignored the first voice. "Are you coming up for Thanksgiving?"

Aaron threw her a questioning glance. "Haven't decided," he said briefly.

"Well, if you do, stop by. My mother owns a gallery on Beacon Hill, just above the Commons." She took a deep breath. "I can give you my address."

"Oh, I'd probably lose it," Aaron replied. He

started to jog again. "If I get up there, I can always find you in the phone book."

Stacy felt a stab of disappointment—and the even sharper pain of humiliation. She had made an offer, and Aaron had just as clearly rejected it. Rejection wasn't something Stacy usually had to deal with. But she wasn't going to show him that she cared. Besides, she *didn't* care. There were better-looking guys—guys with much better taste—just dying to take her out.

"I'm afraid," she said with a toss of her head, "that you can't find me in the book. We're not listed." She picked up her pace. "And I'm afraid I don't make that offer more than once."

She gave Aaron a scornful smile for making such a silly mistake and jogged away, kicking up gravel on the path behind her.

Chapter 3

"Oh, hi, Stacy," Pam Mason said, opening her door. "I've been wanting to talk to you. Come in."

Stacy stepped inside. Pam, a cheerful-looking, slightly plump senior, was the resident adviser for the second floor of Rogers House. Her room, a single, was at the end of the hall, several doors down from suite 2C.

"Have a seat." Pam perched on the bed and combed her fingers through her curly red hair. "What's going on in your life these days?"

Uncomfortably, Stacy sat down in the chair by the window. As RA, Pam was supposed to be a kind of big sister to the freshmen on the floor. Stacy found it a little hard to believe that Pam could relate to her problems, but she knew an RA was the only one who could get her what she wanted at the moment.

"Well," she said, squirming a little, "I want to

change my suite assignment." The humiliating episode last night with Aaron had been the last straw. She couldn't stand to live in the same room with Sam any longer.

Pam looked at her, surprised. "How come?" she asked. "I thought you guys in two C were a good match."

Stacy avoided her gaze. "Yeah, in some ways I guess we are," she admitted. "I mean, we have a good time together." It was true. Roni was a laugh a minute, Sam always knew everything that was happening on campus, and Terry made great hotplate pancakes. But the idea of being in competition with Sam—and losing—was too much. She straightened her shoulders. If Sydney were in this situation, she wouldn't back down; she'd simply *demand* a transfer. "Look, Pam," she said, "it's really very simple. I want to move."

Pam shook her head. "I'm afraid it's not simple at all. Have you read your housing contract?"

"No. Why?"

"Because it says that you have to stay in your suite for an entire semester. You can't transfer in mid-semester unless it's really serious—you know, a life-and-death situation. The Housing Board reviews all requests for room changes, and believe me, they're extremely strict." She looked at Stacy sympathetically. "Why do you want to move?"

Stacy hesitated. Pam was sort of a busybody, but she did always act as if she cared about the girls on her floor. If she knew what had happened, maybe she'd see that it *was* practically a matter of life and death. "To tell the truth, I guess my problem is with Sam," she said.

"What happened?"

Stacy felt herself blushing. "Well, I was interested in a guy, so I called him to ask him to the party we had in our suite." She stopped.

"And then what?"

"Then"—she bit her lip—"Sam took off with him."

"Sam's seeing the guy?"

"Yeah," Stacy said unhappily. "He's over here every day."

Pam hugged her knees. "That must be rough on you. To have to hang around the two of them, I mean."

"Yeah," Stacy said. Good, Pam was beginning to see things her way! "It is. It's hard enough to see *him*, but when I see the two of them together . . ."

"So you figure that moving out would solve things."

Stacy sat forward. "Yes, that's it," she said. "This thing is really making a big mess out of my first semester."

Pam propped her chin on her knees and gave Stacy a direct, thoughtful look. "Is *that* what happened at midterm? With your grades, I mean."

"Well, I . . ." Stacy sat back, frowning. "Which one of my suitemates told you about that?"

"It's not important, Stacy. All I can say is that you're lucky—you've got friends who worry about you."

Stacy sucked in her breath. "If they were really

my friends," she said hotly, "they wouldn't be talking about me behind my back."

Pam gave Stacy another searching look. "Well, is it?"

"Is it what?"

Pam sighed. "Is this situation with Sam the reason you're having trouble?"

Stacy hesitated. Much as she wanted to move out, she couldn't blame her rotten grades on Sam. "No, not really," she admitted. "I just . . . well, I just wasn't into studying for the first few weeks. But things are different now," she added, putting on a confident smile. "I'm working a lot harder."

Pam picked up a bag of potato chips off the table next to the bed. "Do you think you can catch up before finals?" she asked. She held out the bag to Stacy, who shook her head. A single chip had twelve whole calories in it.

"I've already started to work on the stuff I missed," she said.

It was true. She'd gotten up early that morning to run, and then spent a couple of hours reviewing slides for art history. She'd made an appointment to see her music professor the next day, and she'd spent an hour in the pottery studio. "It'll be fine," she added, wanting Pam to believe her, "once I've handed in a little makeup work." She relaxed into a grin. "Nothing to it."

Pam munched a chip and reached for another one. "I love potato chips. You don't eat junk food, do you? I've noticed that you're losing weight," she observed casually. "Are you trying to, or is it a problem. Is the stress of college life getting to you?"

Stacy had to laugh. Since when was willpower a problem? "Gosh, Pam," she said, "most of us could stand to diet once in a while."

"Are you on a diet?"

Stacy shrugged. Why couldn't Pam just accept the fact that she was a slender girl who was bright enough to improve her grades, and that the only reason she was here was because she wanted to move? "Listen, what about my chances for reassignment?" she asked. "Do you think the Housing Board will—"

Pam shook her head. "Sorry, Stacy, not a chance," she replied. "Anyway, it's better in the long run if you hang in there and sort things out. Have you told Sam how you feel about things?"

Stacy stiffened. "You mean you don't want to help me," she said accusingly, getting up.

"I said that the board wouldn't approve your request," Pam corrected her. "I *want* to help you, Stacy—if you'll let me. Listen, I know a really good counselor over in the Student Life office. Maybe you could straighten things out by talking to her. She's helped a lot of people with problems—sex, self-image, relationships, eating disorders, things like that. I'd be glad to introduce—"

Stacy was already at the door. "Thanks," she interrupted, "but I don't have a problem with sex or my self-image. The fact that I'm not always wolfing down pizza or potato chips like most people around here doesn't mean that I have an eating disorder.

And changing suites would solve my relationship problem." She sighed loudly and glanced at her watch. "I have to go. I don't want to be late for my sorority meeting."

As Stacy walked up the azalea-bordered drive in front of the Alpha Pi house, she started thinking about how wonderful it would be to be a junior already, living in the APA house. She wouldn't have to put up with Sam and Aaron or with a nosy RA who wanted to interfere in her personal life.

The members of Alpha Pi were already seated in front of the big brick fireplace at one end of the wood-paneled community room. Stacy sat down on the floor just as Nancy Greer, the president, called the meeting to order and the secretary began to read the minutes. She looked around. Alpha Pi was the smallest and most exclusive of the four sororities at Hawthorne, and the members were among the most popular—and powerful—girls in the college. There was Angie Peterson, for instance, in the front row. Angie was president of the senior class and was going to be at Harvard Law School next year. Her father was president of a bank. Sitting next to her, wearing the distinctive green Honor Board blazer, was Megan Stanford, whose mother owned her own ad agency in Atlanta. These were the people she should be associating with, Stacy told herself.

"Okay, gang," said Nancy Greer, standing up and rapping a small gavel on the table. Nancy was dark-haired and lively-looking, with a great smile. Stacy studied her, especially admiring Nancy's air of easy, confident self-assurance. It must be nice to be so confident that you didn't have to worry about the way you looked or the way people reacted to you.

"I have several announcements," Nancy was saying. "First of all, don't forget about the party on Friday night. It's a cookout followed by a hayride at a farm outside of town, so you should probably wear jeans."

Stacy realized she still needed a date for the party. Should she ask Alex, the guy she had met and danced with at the last party? He certainly was good-looking enough, and he was a Pi Phi—the most popular fraternity on campus, as well as APA's brother fraternity.

"We need cars," Nancy continued, "to drive people out to the farm. Who'll volunteer?"

Stacy put up her hand, and Nancy recognized her. "Thanks, Stacy. How many can fit into your car?"

Stacy frowned. Four was the most she'd ever had in the car. "How many can you put into a Mercedes?" she asked without thinking. Some of the girls whispered to each other enviously, but others whistled and hissed; they obviously thought she was showing off. Behind her, somebody muttered, "God, what *poor* taste." Stacy's face felt like it was on fire, and she twisted in her chair uncomfortably while Nancy took down the names of other volunteers. She couldn't believe she'd been so stupid.

"Okay, next order of business," said Nancy. "We'll be holding our annual elections the week before Thanksgiving. A list of executive council offices is posted on the bulletin board beside the door. If you're interested in running, let the election committee know. The pledges will vote for a pledge representative. It's a great way for a pledge to get involved and be a real leader and, I hope all you pledges will think about running. Even campaigning for the position should be fun."

APA pledge representative to the executive council—maybe *that* was the kind of change Stacy had been looking for. If she were pledge representative, she'd get to know the most important people in APA fast. And she had campaigning blood in her veins, didn't she? Her father had been elected for three terms as a state senator, and he was about to be elected to a fourth. And her mother had been president of her sorority at Vassar. She began to smile to herself. Sam could have silly little Aaron, Terry could have her straight A's, and Pam could sit in her room minding other people's business. Stacy had much better things to do. In no time at all, she was going to be one of the most well-known people in Hawthorne College.

Chapter 4

Thrilled with her new plan, Stacy walked quickly back to the suite after the sorority meeting. Preoccupied, she bumped right into Aaron and Sam when she opened the door.

"Hi, Stacy," Sam said, slinging her bookbag over her shoulder. "Listen, somebody named Roger called, from your English class. His number's on the notepad by the phone."

"Thanks," Stacy said, managing a smile. Roger. That must be the blond guy who had smiled at her yesterday after class, the one with the Beta sweatshirt.

"Oh, and your mom called," Sam added. "She wants you to call her."

"Did she say what she wanted?" Stacy asked with a glance at Aaron. Sure, he was good-looking, but Roger was just as good-looking. And Alex was better looking than either of them. Sam could definitely have Aaron. Anyway, now that Stacy was going to run for office, it wouldn't pay to be seen with guys who weren't in the best fraternities.

"Something about Thanksgiving," Sam replied.

Stacy nodded. "Okay," she said. "I'll call her."

But not right away. Sydney was always changing her mind and would probably change it three more times before the holidays. Besides, she still had to go to the library and work on her overdue English paper for Dr. Marshall, anyway. One of her mother's lectures wouldn't exactly put her in the mood for that.

Terry came out of her room just as Sam and Aaron left. "Have you had supper yet?" she asked. "How about a hamburger at The Eatery after you call your mom?"

"No, thanks," Stacy said. "I'm not hungry." That wasn't exactly true. She hadn't eaten since lunch, and she felt a few hunger pangs. But there was some yogurt in the refrigerator, and anyway, she was tired of Terry's nagging—especially after her meeting with Pam. She gave Terry a pointed look. "I saw Pam today," she said. "She told me somebody had talked to her about my grade report."

Terry colored. "I . . . it was me," she said. "I've been worried about you, Stacy. I wish we could talk about—"

"And I wish you'd keep your nose in your book and your mouth shut," Stacy said in an icy tone. "I don't need your help, and I don't need you talking about me behind my back. To Pam or anybody else."

She looked up. There were tears in Terry's eyes, and Stacy felt a stab of remorse. What was her problem? How could she be so mean and insensitive to somebody who just wanted to help? "I'm sorry, Terry," she mumbled. "I . . . I guess I'm just not used to living with people who pay so much attention to my life. I've basically been living on my own the past few years."

Terry nodded. "I understand—I guess," she said with a shy smile. "I just have a hard time figuring out how to help without making people mad. I didn't mean to offend you."

Stacy looked toward the refrigerator. It was getting hard to ignore her growling stomach. "I guess I *will* have something to eat," she said. "I left some yogurt here yesterday."

"Yogurt?" Terry asked just as Stacy opened the refrigerator. "Oh, gosh, Stace, I didn't know that was *your* yogurt. I ate it."

Stacy stared at the empty shelf. Suddenly she was so hungry she felt shaky, as if she might faint.

Terry took out a bowl. "Listen, let me make you a tuna-salad sandwich."

"But I don't *want* a sandwich," Stacy protested. She sat down on the sofa. "I don't eat bread."

Terry looked at her. "Then how about some tuna salad *without* the bread? Here," she said, thrusting a plate in front of Stacy. "Eat it." She shook her head. "You know, Stacy, what you need is a *mother*."

Stacy took a bite of tuna salad. It tasted good. "I guess I'm not very used to having a mother around," she admitted with a little laugh. "Sydney's never been the mothering type."

"Yeah." Terry laughed, too. "Sometimes I think that the great parent lottery in the sky doesn't always award kids the kinds of parents they deserve. *My* father spends his weekends in the neighborhood bar, and my mom spends *her* weekends wishing he'd come home." She shrugged and picked up the milk. "I figure I deserve better, and the fact that I didn't get it really depresses me sometimes. But I can't let it drag me down. Want a glass of milk?"

Stacy nodded and took the milk. She'd never heard Terry talk about her family before. And she definitely never imagined that Terry might relate to her problems with Sydney and Jason. "Uh, Terry?" she said. "Thanks."

"Don't mention it," Terry said cheerfully. "Anytime you want to talk, or need a sandwich, I'm here. Just call me mom," she said, laughing.

The next afternoon, Stacy finally finished her English paper. It was a essay on Shakespeare's *Othello*, liberally borrowed from a paper she'd written at Elizabeth Deere. She congratulated herself on having had the foresight to bring those old papers with her. She'd gotten an A on that one, and Professor Marshall was bound to like it, too.

When she finished copying the paper so that it was legible, she walked the two blocks to Grove Street to drop it off at the typing service. Along the way, she met Roger, the guy from her English class, who walked with her as far as the gym. She'd been right.

He was a Beta, and he wanted to ask her to a Friday night party. She shook her head and said no, she'd promised to drive her car to the Alpha Pi cookout. Actually, she was glad to have an excuse. Roger did look like he'd just stepped out out of the pages of a catalog, but unfortunately, he seemed to have a personality to match. In fact, she thought as they walked and kicked away all the fallen leaves, talking about how well he'd done in Hawthorne's last few football games, he was about as boring and conceited as you could get. Still, he *was* a Beta.

When she left the typing service, she hurried back toward the Fine Arts Complex. It was nearly 3:15, and she was due to talk to Dr. Ross, her music appreciation professor, at 3:30. She'd dressed carefully, in a slim beige skirt and a pin-striped brown-and-white blouse. She wanted to look like a serious student—for the next hour anyway.

Dr. Ross's office was on the second floor of the music wing of the Fine Arts Complex, with a window overlooking the lake. "So *that's* why I didn't know who you were at first," he said when she introduced herself. "You're the elusive Stacy Swanson."

"I guess I *did* miss a few classes before midterm," Stacy admitted, recalling all her successful win-the-teachers-over strategies from prep school. You didn't want to invent an excuse they could check, like a sick grandmother or a bout of tonsilitis. You had to come clean, confess your sins, and then convince them that you truly wanted to improve—with their teaching as your inspiration, of course. "But I plan to do better in the second half," she added penitently, lowering her eyes and putting on her most contrite look. "Much better."

"Oh?" Dr. Ross opened his grade book. "Exactly *how* much better?"

Stacy frowned. She wasn't sure she liked the tone of his voice. "Well I'm not going to miss any more classes, that's for sure. I mean, I . . . I'd like to get a B, at least," she said hopefully. "Or maybe even an A." After all, it *was* music appreciation. *Everybody* would get A's and B's.

Dr. Ross closed his grade book. "I see," he said. He leaned back in his chair and looked at her through half-closed eyes. "Well, then, Miss Swanson, you are going to be very busy. You have four quizzes to make up, a five-page paper to write, and two concerts to attend."

Stacy gasped. "But I *can't* have missed that much!"

Dr. Ross pushed his grade book across his desk. "It's all there," he said. "Take a look if you want to."

Stacy opened the book. The row beside her name was almost empty, and at the end was a big red F. She swallowed.

"I guess I missed more than I thought," she admitted. "Is . . . is it possible that you could . . . well, maybe just not count one or two of the quizzes? I really and truly want to make up as much as I can, but that's a lot, and if I get zeros for those . . ."

Dr. Ross stood up and put his hands in his pockets. His shoulders were rounded, and he looked almost sad. "Miss Swanson," he said, "I have been blessed by the fates with the joyful task of teaching at Hawthorne College. I love my work. I love music. I love my students."

"Yes, I know," Stacy said. What was he leading up to? "I think you're a very good—"

Dr. Ross held up his hand. "Last week," he went on, "the chairman of my department informed me that I love my students just a little *too* much. The computer has revealed that, in comparison with other professors, I give too many A's. Word has it on campus that Music 105 is a"—his mouth wrinkled distastefully—"Mickey Mouse course, and that Professor Ross is an easy A."

"Oh, but I don't—" Stacy began.

Dr. Ross silenced her with a mournful look. "So you see, Miss Swanson, while I might wish, out of the kindness of my heart, to forget these assignments" —he coughed—"I cannot. If you want to receive more than a D, you will have to make up all of the work." He looked at her sternly. "*All* of it."

Stacy walked out of Dr. Ross's office shaking her head in disbelief. She couldn't decide whether Dr. Ross was for real or whether she had just been conned by an expert. She sighed. Quizzes, concerts, and a five-page paper—in addition to art history makeup, another English paper, and the pottery project she had to finish! It was impossible—especially now that she had her heart set on being elected to the APA Executive Council. How was she going to find time for everything?

* * *

The pottery studio was located on the first floor of the art wing of the Fine Arts Complex, across from the music wing. Stacy stopped at her locker and pulled out a pair of clay-stained white coveralls and a blue T-shirt and went into the women's restroom to change. Then she got her clay, her plastic bucket, and her tools and took everything to one of the electric wheels. It was nearly four, and the studio was deserted.

Actually, Stacy thought, of all her classes, she liked ceramics the most. She hunched over the wheel intently, forearms on her thighs, elbows tucked against her sides, picturing in her mind the profile of the mug she was making. For her project, she was going to make a set of six mugs. Three of them had already been fired in the kiln and now they had to be glazed. If she threw the other three today, she could glaze them next week. She was sure that Ms. Lowry, the instructor, would like her project, and she'd probably give her an A. No need to con the professor this time.

Stacy was so absorbed in her work that she didn't notice the boy who was sweeping his way across the studio until he was standing right next to her.

"Hey," he said loudly, "would you move your foot?"

"What?" Stacy turned to look at him, and her hand hit the clay, knocking it off center. "Darn it," she said, stopping the wheel.

"Sorry," said the boy.

Stacy took a good look at him as he spoke. He

was tall, with red hair, blue-green eyes, and a smudge of sandy freckles. He was wearing a pair of well-worn jeans and a blue denim work shirt with the sleeves rolled up.

"I asked once before, but I guess you didn't hear me," he said, speaking with a slow southern drawl. He looked down at the lump of misshapen clay. "Is it ruined?"

Stacy poked her finger at it. "Of course," she said in a snobbish tone. "I can use the clay again, but I'll have to wedge it first."

"Wedge it?" he asked. "What's that?"

Stacy looked up, annoyed. "You work in a pottery studio and you don't know what wedging is?"

The boy grinned. "Actually, mostly what I do around here is mix clay and haul pots to the kiln and sweep up. I'm a gofer, not an artist."

"A gopher?"

The boy's grin grew wider. "As in go-for this, go-for that," he explained. "It's my work-study job."

"Oh," Stacy said. She threw the second lump of clay on the wheel and began to work. "Wedging is kneading the clay. You do it to get air bubbles out."

"Mind if I watch?" he asked. "Usually when I'm here nobody's working, and I've never watched somebody actually make a pot."

"I'm sure you'll be bored," Stacy said. "And I'm only making a mug, not a pot. Nothing elaborate."

"If I get bored, I'll go back to sweeping," the boy said. "But I don't think I'll get *that* bored." They both laughed.

So for the next half hour, while Stacy threw three

mugs, he watched, not saying anything to disturb her. When she was finished with the last one, he said, "You really seem to know what you're doing, I like the way your hands move with the clay—you really get into it."

Stacy carried her finished mugs to the drying shelf. "Oh, I'm just a beginner," she replied. His compliment made her a little uncomfortable. It seemed sort of personal.

"Transfer student?"

"No, freshman."

"Really? You look older. Where are you from?" he asked, following her over to the sink and then back to the wheel.

Stacy stopped and turned to him. "I'm from Boston," she said, beginning to feel a little strange. Who was this person, and why was she having this conversation? If this was a work-study job, maybe she could get one—the hours were great.

"Yeah, I thought so." The boy nodded, his eyes twinkling. "It's the way you say your R's. 'Pahk the cah in Bah-stan.'"

Stacy picked up her tools. "From the way you say *your* R's," she retorted, "I'd guess you're from the South—the *deep* South."

"Well, if you guessed that, you'd be right." He propped his broom against the wall. "Give you a hand with that?" He took her tools. "Actually," he added, following her into the hall, "I'm from Hawthorne Springs. Before that, my family lived in an even smaller town in south Georgia."

"Mmm." Stacy opened her locker. He was kind of cute, with those blue-green eyes and sandy freckles, and his persistence was flattering. But if she'd had any interest in him, that was the end of it. A work-study student who was not only southern, but lived in Hawthorne Springs . . . it wasn't the kind of company you kept if you wanted to get elected to an office at APA. "Do you ever get bored living here?" she asked pointedly.

The boy put down her tools, laughing. "Yeah, you might say it's boring sometimes," he said. "And I suppose it's kind of provincial, too. But I've always liked small towns. My cousin lives in Atlanta, and when I visit there I notice that the people aren't as neighborly as they are here." He shrugged. "*You* must have wanted to be in a small town," he remarked, "or you'd have gone to Boston University or Columbia or someplace like that."

"Well, not exactly." Stacy reached for her clothes, which were hanging in the locker. If she tried to explain why she'd come to Hawthorne, he'd never understand. "If you don't mind, I need to change. I have to be somewhere soon."

"Yeah, I guess I'd better get back to work," the boy said. He offered his hand. "My name is Pete," he said. "Pete Young. Do you come around the studio very often?"

"Probably not as often as I should," Stacy said, thinking of the work she still had to do on her incomplete project. She turned and headed for the women's room.

"Hey," Pete called, "you didn't tell me your name!"

Stacy turned at the doorway. Pete was standing in the hall, hands in his pockets, watching her. "No," she said, "I guess I didn't, did I?" She went in and closed the door.

Chapter 5

Before Stacy left the art wing, she stopped by a drinking fountain and swallowed a couple of diet pills. Then she walked toward the Commons dining hall, it was after five, and the chilly evening breeze rippled the lake. She started thinking of what was next on her "Things to Accomplish" list. She was trying to plot campaign strategies, but she couldn't get that red-haired guy in the pottery studio out of her head.

Pete. Pete Young. She had probably been rude to him—no, that was wrong: she *had* been rude. She could have given him her name, but she had felt like being coy. There wasn't any point to it anyway, she told herself. It wasn't as if she were interested in him. Absolutely not. Although he *was* kind of cute— well, he had a cute grin, and his eyes were nice, and she liked the casual, easy way he held himself. But those clothes—and that accent! They *had* to go. Well, what did she expect? What could she have in common with a guy from Hawthorne Springs? She wasn't being stuck up, she told herself, just realistic.

Stacy pulled open the door to the Commons and went into the serving area, making her way to the cooler at the back of the cafeteria area where the yogurt was kept. Then she went to the salad bar for a bowl of raw cauliflower and broccoli. Even if she ate half a pound of the stuff, it would only be about fifty calories. At this rate, she ought to lose that bulge in no time. She went to stand in the checkout line.

"I don't know why *you're* dieting," said a voice said behind her. "You've got an absolutely fabulous figure. You make us all green with envy."

Stacy turned around. It was Nancy Greer, holding a dish of lettuce and cottage cheese and a cup of black coffee.

"Oh, hi, Nancy," Stacy said, pleased at the compliment. The clerk punched her meal plan, and she waited while Nancy looked for hers. "I'm really glad I ran into you," Stacy said. "Do you have a minute?"

Nancy glanced at her watch. "Not much more than a minute," she said. "I just got out of a late class, and I'm on my way to an executive council meeting." She nodded toward a nearby empty table. "Over there okay?"

They sat down, and Stacy opened her yogurt. "Actually," she said, "it's the executive council that I want to talk to you about." She dipped her spoon into the yogurt. "I'd like to run as pledge representative."

Nancy smiled. "Why do you want to run?" she asked, taking a bite of her cottage cheese.

Stacy shrugged. "Because I want to get more involved in Alpha Pi," she said. "I think I'd get more out of the sorority. And my father's in politics—I've worked in a couple of his campaigns. It'd be fun." As she talked, she began to feel even more enthusiastic about it.

"Hey, that's great," said Nancy. "The three of you ought to make for an interesting race."

"The three of us?" Stacy asked.

"Right," Nancy said. "Rachel Ross and Laura Williams have already filed with the committee."

Stacy picked up a piece of cauliflower and began to nibble on it, trying to remember her father's campaigns. "How do you think I can let people know . . . well, who I am, what I've done—stuff like that?"

Nancy thought for a minute. "Well, since we've got three really different candidates, maybe it would be good if they made a presentation to the pledges." She sipped her coffee. "What do you think?"

"Sounds good," Stacy said. "It would give people a chance to find out who's who."

Nancy stood up and took a last gulp of her coffee. "I wish I could talk longer," she said, putting her cup down, "but it's time for the meeting. See you later," she called over her shoulder.

"Who was that?" Roni asked curiously, coming up

behind Stacy. She sat down and piled her books on the table.

"Hi, Roni," Stacy said. "That was Nancy Greer, the Alpha Pi president. We were talking about the campaign."

"Campaign?" Roni stretched and yawned, running her hands through her hair. "You're running for something?"

"For pledge representative," Stacy replied. "Listen, Roni, you wouldn't believe what happened this afternoon," she said, giggling, and told Roni about her music professor. "It looks like his sins were found out by the computer."

Roni laughed. "That reminds me of the time back in high school when I flunked PE."

"*You* flunked PE?" asked Terry, sitting down beside Roni. "I always thought you must be really good in PE. I mean, you're a dancer, aren't you?"

"Yeah, but this was *volleyball*," Roni said, shuddering. "I mean, I was doing okay in everything else that semester, but there was no way I could handle volleyball, especially at seven-thirty in the morning. And the teacher—you wouldn't *believe* this teacher. She acted like she'd just graduated from West Point." She leaned back, beginning to laugh. "And she had this whistle, this really *obnoxious* whistle, that she was always blowing at people whenever they did something she didn't like. But we fixed that."

"Oh, yeah?" Stacy asked, interested. "How'd you do that?"

"I got some girls together, and we sneaked into the teacher's office and poured glue in her whistle. And the next time she blew it, she puffed until her face turned red, and it still wouldn't work." Roni giggled. "And while we were at it, we glued the pages of her grade book together."

"Her grade book!" cried Terry. "Roni, that's . . . that's almost *illegal*. I mean, you could get into lots of trouble doing that."

Roni shrugged. "Yeah, maybe—but that's what makes it fun, isn't it? Anyway, after that things *really* heated up. She got mad because everybody in the class laughed at her and nobody would tell who glued up her whistle, so she flunked the entire class. And then the parents got into the act, and she had to go before the board of this really ritzy private school and show them her glued-up whistle and her grade book and explain why she flunked everybody." Roni looked smug. "My folks figured I was being unjustly punished, so they didn't hold the F against me, and the teacher had to get another job at the end of the semester."

Stacy grinned, shaking her head. "Looks like I should have hired you as a consultant before I tried to figure out how to get my grades changed," she said. She stood up. "I've got to go to the music lab and study for a quiz."

After Stacy had listened to Beethoven's Ninth Symphony, she was in an even better mood. The lab was closing in a few minutes, so she started back to Rogers House around the lake. Again she found herself thinking about the boy she'd met in the pottery studio. She could have kicked herself for being so rude. She should have found a nicer way of letting him know that she wasn't interested. Suddenly she heard something that sounded like mewing, as if a kitten were crying. She looked behind a tree where the noise was coming from. It *was* a kitten! A fuzzy white kitten with a gray masklike patch on its face and a stumpy tail that trembled when he rubbed her ankles. It was so cute and helpless that it made Stacy's heart leap.

"What are you doing out here all by yourself, alone in the dark?" she asked, dropping her books to pick him up. He purred happily and thrust his wet paws against her face.

She held the kitten at arm's length. "What am I going to do with you?" she asked him. "I can't just let you go—you'll starve." She looked at the gray mask across his face and giggled. "Even if you are a bandit."

The kitten meowed.

"Bandit," she said, laughing softly. "Yes, that's it. You held me up and forced me to capture you. Bandit."

"Oh, hi, Stacy," Terry said from the sofa where she was reading. "Listen, your mom called. She says it's the second time and you should call her. And somebody named Alex called, too. He . . . " She stopped. "What in the world is that fuzzy thing under your arm?"

"This 'fuzzy thing,'" Stacy replied, putting the kitten on the floor, "is Bandit. He's a kitten."

"I thought so," Terry said. "I could tell by the tail and whiskers." She looked at the cat over her glasses.

"But what is he doing?" She stopped and then sighed. "Forget I asked," she said, taking her glasses off. "Better get a paper towel."

Stacy giggled. "Oops I guess kittens do that sometimes," she said, cleaning up after Bandit. "He needs a litter box."

"*What?*" Terry asked incredulously. "Stacy, we all love cats, but you can't possibly plan to *keep* this kitten!"

Stacy lay down on her stomach and watched Bandit exploring under the sofa. "Why not?" she asked. "Why can't I keep him? He doesn't seem to have fleas, and I'm sure I can house-train him in a hurry."

"You can't keep the kitten," Terry said patiently, "because it's against dorm rules. Besides, Stacy, what do you want a kitten *for?*"

"What would anybody want a kitten for?" asked Stacy. "Because he's cute and cuddly. Because he needs somebody to love him. Is there a better reason?" Bandit poked his head out from under the sofa and blinked at her, whiskers covered with dust. "Anyway, nobody will notice. He can live in my bedroom." She got up and went to the refrigerator, taking out a carton of milk. "Is this your milk?"

"No, it's Sam's," Terry said. "But you shouldn't feed—"

"I'm sure Sam won't mind," Stacy mumbled. She set a bowl of milk in front of Bandit. "He's hungry," she said, watching him lap the milk. "I wonder if he likes canned cat food."

"Oh, God, Stacy," Terry groaned, "you can't be

serious about this! You'll get us all in trouble. That's the last thing I need—I have enough to worry about."

"Hi, everybody!" Roni yelled, bursting into the room. "You'll never guess what . . ." She saw Bandit and let out a little yelp, leaning over to pet him. "Oh, isn't he *adorable*?" she crooned. "How precious! Whose is he?"

"Mine," Stacy said. "I found him, over by the lake."

"He's nobody's," Terry said firmly. "He's a stray."

Stacy stood up. Bandit had lapped up the last of the milk and was methodically washing his ear with one white paw. "He's mine," she repeated with a look at Terry.

"Can't you reason with her?" Terry pleaded with Roni. "She'd going to get in trouble keeping a cat in the suite. We'll *all* be in trouble."

Roni shrugged and pulled off her scarf. "It's Stacy's cat," she said. "If she wants to get in trouble, it's her business. I seriously doubt that we'll get in trouble just because our suitemate brought a cat home. You worry too much, Terry. Relax. Nobody's going to jail—yet." She grinned mischievously.

The telephone rang, and Roni reached for it. "It's for you," she told Stacy. "It's your mother."

Stacy took the phone and sat down on the floor, with Bandit trying to crawl under her legs. Laughing, she said, "Stop that, Bandit!"

"What?" Sydney asked. "Is that you, Stacy? Stacy?"

Stacy pulled Bandit onto her lap. "Hello, Sydney," she said. "I have a new cat."

"A cat? You can keep pets in the dorm?"

Stacy chuckled and gently pulled Bandit's stumpy tail. "What they don't know won't hurt them," she said. "To coin a phrase. How are you?" she asked. "What's up for Thanksgiving? Are we still going to the lodge?"

"That's why I'm calling, Stacy," Sydney said. She cleared her throat. "The plans for Thanksgiving have changed. I hope you won't mind, but—"

"We're staying in Boston?" Stacy asked. There was silence. "New York, maybe?" She could shop in New York.

There was another silence. "Actually," Sydney said, "we're going to the Serengeti."

"The Serengeti?" Stacy gulped. "Do you mean the African restaurant or the African region? Sydney, I can't possibly get there and back over Thanksgiving."

"I know you can't, dear," Sydney said patiently. "And as it turns out, I really wouldn't want you to. You see, David and I are going to be married, and this is going to be our honeymoon. We're very much in love, dear." There was another silence. "I hope you understand why we need to be alone."

Stacy didn't say anything for a minute. Then she managed a little laugh. "I see," she said. "Yes, I guess it would be sort of awkward."

"Of course, we'd love to have you," Sydney said with a little cough, "but it's out of the question. We'll be gone for three months or so."

"Oh," Stacy said, trying to control her voice. She was *not* going to cry. "You'll be gone over Christmas, too, then."

"But you'll hardly know I'm gone. It's only three months—hardly a real vacation," Sydney was saying. "Your father will be around, of course. And he might even have some time for you, after the election." There was sarcasm in her throaty laugh. "In fact, he'll probably even let you star in one of his famous parties. 'Beautiful daughter home from college,' that sort of thing."

"Probably," Stacy agreed, trying to ignore the sarcasm. She wondered if all divorced parents sniped at each other as nastily as hers did. "Anyway," she said, "congratulations. On getting married, I mean." She'd only met David once, but he seemed a lot like the other two men her mother had married after the divorce. They'd usually managed to be conveniently away on business when Stacy came home for a holiday.

"No, dear," her mother corrected her. "That's not the way it's done. You congratulate the *groom*. You give the bride your best wishes."

"Oh. Well then, congratulate David for me. And best wishes to you."

"Thanks." There was a pause. "How are your studies going?"

"Oh, okay," Stacy said. "I'm catching up." She pulled Bandit closer to her. Would this horrible phone call never end? "Listen, Sydney, I have to go," she said. "Enjoy the Serengeti. Give my love to the giraffes."

Stacy hung up abruptly as her mother was saying, "Don't be angry, I—" She'd had enough bad news for one day.

"The Serengeti?" Roni said incredulously. "In Africa?" She shook her head. "God, you'll *never* make it back in time for finals."

"I'm not going." Stacy swallowed the lump in her throat. "Sydney and David are."

"David?" Terry asked. "Who's David?"

"The guy she's marrying," Stacy replied. She looked down at Bandit. "Her fourth husband." She tried to smile, but it didn't come off very well. "My mother sort of has this thing for getting married. Unfortunately, she also seems to have a thing for getting divorced."

"Oh," Terry said. "Well. That's too bad."

"Yeah, well," Roni spoke up, "you're welcome to come to Atlanta for Thanksgiving." She chuckled. "I'm sure my parents have plans for a traditional holiday, but we can definitely find something *untraditional* to do."

"Or you could come to Philadelphia," Terry added. "It might be different from what you're used to, but . . ."

Stacy shook her head. "Thanks," she said, "but my father wants me to spend the holiday with him."

"In Boston?" Roni asked. "Fabulous."

"Yes," Stacy replied. "I'll probably have a lot more fun with my father, anyway. The most fascinating people turn up at his parties—prime ministers and Broadway stars and artists." She smiled.

"You're lucky," Roni said enviously. "My father's

as square as they come." She paused. "Maybe I ought to come home with you."

Terry glanced at Bandit. "Well," she said, "that settles it. This cat will have to go—nobody'll be here to take care of him."

"You're right," Stacy said. She picked Bandit up. "He will have to go—with me. I'll get a cat carrier." She rubbed his furry face against hers. "You won't love flying, but you'll love Boston—and then when we come back, you can help me get ready for finals."

Terry rolled her eyes. "Does he know anything about biology?"

Chapter 6

Stacy woke up several times during the night with Bandit on the pillow, purring hard. But she didn't mind. Every time she woke, she fell asleep again almost immediately, a loving Bandit snuggled against her. She was awake at 6:15 and climbing into her white running shorts when Sam woke up with a startled screech.

Stacy whirled around. "What's wrong?"

Sam was sitting bolt upright in bed, rubbing her eyes and staring at the furry heap on Stacy's pillow. "Your kitten!" she gasped. "It's washing its face!"

Bandit yawned an enormous kitten yawn. "Of course he washes his face," Stacy said, laughing. "That's because he's not stuffed. He's real."

"Oh," Sam said with a relieved sigh. "That's good. For a minute I thought I was hallucinating." She sat on the edge of the bed and stretched over to touch her toes, her long hair falling forward. "Where'd he come from?"

Stacy shrugged and pulled on a green Hawthorne T-shirt. "Who knows?" she replied. "I found him by the lake last night."

Sam stripped out of her pajamas and went into the bathroom to brush her teeth. "He's cute," she said through the door. "What are you going to do with him?"

"Keep him," Stacy said briefly. She sat down on the edge of the bed and fastened on her wrist weights.

"Keep him?" Sam stuck her head through the door, toothbrush in hand.

Stacy picked up her brush and ran it through her hair. "Do you have any objections?"

"Well, no—other than the fact that it's against dorm rules." Sam came back into the room and pulled on her blue sweatpants. "What'll happen when Pam finds out?"

"She won't," Stacy said, "unless somebody tells her." She leaned over and kissed Bandit's white ear. "Be a good boy," she told him. "I'll be back after I do two laps."

"Stacy," Sam said, pulling her sweatshirt over her head, "how about running together?"

"Oh?" Stacy said archly. "I thought you ran with Aaron." The minute she'd said it, she wished she hadn't. She had decided that Aaron wasn't worth getting upset over after all. And she really didn't like fighting with Sam.

There was a silence. "Stacy, can't we make

peace?" Sam asked miserably. "Cold war is *so* awful." She paused. "I just wish we could start all over again."

Stacy hesitated, looking at Sam. "How about this morning?" she asked tentatively. "Would you like to do a couple of laps?"

Sam's face lit up. "Really?"

Stacy nodded. "Yeah," she said softly. "Really."

Sam grabbed her hairbrush and began to pull her hair back into a ponytail. "Hey," she said, grinning, "this is great. Someone to share the sweat and agony with."

"Not to mention the pain and humiliation," Stacy added, "when I beat you to the lake." Both girls pushed and shoved each other on their way out the door, laughing.

Stacy skipped lunch that noon so she could get to the typing service and pick up her English paper before she saw Dr. Marshall. The paper hadn't turned out as long as she'd hoped, but it looked nice. Even the title sounded important: "Love and Death in Shakespeare's *Othello*." She hoped that Dr. Marshall would be so impressed by the title and the typing job that he'd overlook the fact that it was two pages short.

She tucked the paper into her notebook and walked to the English building to find Dr. Marshall. After her talk yesterday with Dr. Ross, she'd decided to try a different strategy with Dr. Marshall. So this morning, when she changed for class, she'd put on her clingiest sweater, a white one, and her tight black skirt, slit above the knee. There was more than one way to deal with this problem, she'd told herself as she put on her makeup, adding extra mascara and a touch of her new—very expensive—perfume. Once she'd had a problem with a history class at Elizabeth Deere, and her handsome teacher had been very understanding. It had only taken a few smiles from her, and a few undeserved compliments, and he'd forgiven the quiz she owed him.

Dr. Marshall was in his late twenties, and he'd mentioned in class that this was his first year of teaching. He seemed to like his students, and Stacy wasn't surprised when he remembered her name. He was wearing a tweed jacket with leather elbow patches and smoking a fragrant pipe.

"Ah, yes, Miss Swanson," he said, taking his pipe out of his mouth and sitting at his desk. "I'm glad you've come to see me. I was getting worried about you."

Stacy sat on the closest chair to his desk and crossed her legs. Her skirt fell open just above the knee. "Worried about me?" she asked. She looked up at him, batting her lashes.

"Yes." He grinned. "You're the only student with the distinction of being *two* papers behind the class."

Stacy opened her notebook. "Here's one," she said, putting the paper on his desk. "I'm sorry to be late with it," she said, "but I've had several family problems, and . . ." She smiled hesitantly. "I hate to ask, but do you think you might just *forgive* the other paper? I promise to do a much better job in class from now on, but . . ." She smiled again and sniffed.

"My," she said softly, "but that's *wonderful* pipe to-bacco."

Dr. Marshall stood up and tapped his pipe into an ashtray. For a minute he didn't say anything. Then he put his hands in his pockets and went to the window, where he stood with his back to Stacy.

"My dear Miss Swanson," he said gently, "I'm afraid that just won't work."

Stacy frowned. "Won't work?" she asked. "What won't work? I . . . I don't understand."

He turned to face her. "Of course you do," he said, "you understand perfectly. You'll have to turn in your other late paper, and it will be graded down for every day it's late." He looked at her intently. "And no, thanks; whatever you're selling, I'm not buying."

Stacy sucked in a deep breath. It sounded awful, the way he put it. "I . . . I didn't mean . . ." she stammered, her face bright red. "It wasn't what you think."

"Good. I'm glad I'm wrong." Dr. Marshall strode back to his desk and picked up the paper. He glanced through it quickly, reading the first and last paragraphs, and then handed it to her. "I'd like you to expand this argument by about two pages." He picked up his pipe again and began to fill it. "I'll expect it Monday morning."

Stacy took the paper, her face burning, and turned toward the door. She had never felt so embarrassed and foolish in her entire life.

"Miss Swanson," Dr. Marshall said gently. "Stacy."

Reluctantly, Stacy turned around, not wanting to look at him.

He smiled. "There's a more appropriate way to get the grade you want. It's called studying. I recommend it highly."

Stacy couldn't get out of there fast enough.

Chapter 7

By the time Stacy got back to suite 2C, the enormous weight of her own stupidity made her feel so small that she felt she could almost creep under the door without opening it. How could she have so incredibly *stupid*? What was she thinking of? What would she have done if Dr. Marshall *had* responded to her flirting? And how was she going to face him in class next week?

Roni was in the living room wearing a silver-and-black leotard and doing strenuous aerobics to a very loud tape. Stacy gave her a brief wave, then went into her bedroom and shut the door. She was immediately accosted by Bandit, who rubbed against her ankles, mewing hungrily.

Stacy opened the bag of groceries she had picked up earlier that day. "Let's see," she said, "what kind of treat do we have for a kitty who's been good all day?" She took out a foil packet of cat food and opened it into Bandit's saucer. Overcome with excitement, he scrambled over to the saucer and began to gobble. Forgetting her troubles, Stacy chuckled at his comic awkwardness, then went into the living room to get him some milk.

Roni propped a foot on the back of a chair and began doing leg pulls as Stacy poured out Bandit's milk. "Do you think the kitten's worth getting in trouble over?" she asked casually.

Stacy put the carton away and sat down on the coffee table. "What do you mean?"

"Some things are worth doing, no matter what. Even when they make your parents get mad and want to kick you out." Roni arched her back to reach for her ankle. "Some things aren't."

Stacy pulled her knees under her chin and looked at Roni. "Have your parents ever kicked you out?"

"Not exactly." Roni changed legs. "It was more like I decided to leave. But my mother was so upset that I went back. It wasn't worth it."

Stacy thought for a minute. "I've never really wanted to leave. But I've never been sure that they wanted me, or had time for me. In fact, a lot of times I've been sure that they *didn't* have time for me." She laughed sadly. "I can always tell when they're feeling guilty about it, though."

Roni tossed her hair back. "Oh, yeah? How?"

"They *buy* me something," Stacy said. "How do you think I got all that jewelry? And that car?" She stood up and walked to the French doors, looking out. "Jason promised we'd go to London for graduation. We were going to do the museums, Buckingham Palace—you know, like real tourists. But he had to cancel."

Roni grinned. "So you got the car." She shook her head. "I don't know. Given the choice between a trip with my father and a new Mercedes, I'd take the Mercedes."

Stacy grinned back. It was the first time she'd ever told anybody about the car. "Yeah," she said, "but your father isn't Jason. I mean, he's really terrific." She shook her head. "I wonder if I'm ever going to find a guy half as terrific as Jason."

"Is that why you keep trying out so many different guys?" Roni chuckled. "You've had more experience than any girl I've ever met." She bent over and grasped both ankles. "I loved that story you told us about being marooned with the boat captain on that island and being rescued by the Coast Guard. And going out with an Arabian sheikh—what a great story." She picked up the towel again. "So how about this guy you're going out with tonight?"

Stacy shrugged. Alex had called earlier in the week, so she had invited him to the cookout because it was better than going alone. "Too early to tell yet," she said. "We'll see."

Alex didn't mind riding to the party with the carful of girls Stacy had to transport. In fact, he seemed to be enjoying it very much, Stacy thought as she listened to him flirting with the girl next to him, sitting almost on his lap. But she couldn't complain about the attention he was paying to *her*. He'd kissed her warmly when she'd picked him up at the Pi Phi house, and she'd already pushed his hand off her thigh once as they drove. In fact, she was glad *she* was driving, because the beer in his hand obviously wasn't his first.

There were eight of them, crammed into her Mercedes, laughing and joking. Alex was looking extremely preppy and very cool in his tweedy gray sweater and jeans. Actually, she thought, he looked a little like Michael J. Fox, with his arrogant grin and a touch of cockiness. Next to Alex was a plumpish pledge named Brenda, who lived on the first floor of Rogers and spoke with a broad Texas accent. Brenda started every other sentence with "y'all," and she kept giggling and putting her arm across the seat behind Alex. Next to her, with a beer, was Sandy, an RA in Rogers. Sandy's beer kept sloshing on Brenda, which made her giggle even more. There were four in the backseat, too—two girls Stacy didn't really know and their dates.

The farm was about fifteen miles from campus. When they got there it was already dark, and a large group was gathered around a roaring bonfire. One of the guys was sweeping off an area for dancing, and somebody else was setting up speakers for the rock band.

"Hi, Stacy," Nancy said, coming up to her. "Hey, the executive council went for the idea of a meet-the-candidates session for the pledges. We're going to have it next week, Saturday morning."

"Great! I'll be there," Stacy promised with a smile.

"The band's not here yet," Alex said, leaning closer to Stacy, "and it's too early to eat. How about a walk?"

Stacy glanced around. Everybody was just standing around, drinking beer from the keg. Alex had gotten himself another beer, and he was looking less handsome by the minute. In fact, his face was a little flushed, and he had a strange look in his eye. For a moment, Pete Young's innocent, kind face appeared before Stacy's eyes, but she quickly chased it away. Sure, he was nice—but he wasn't her type.

"I'd love to go for a walk," she said, "as long as we don't get lost. It's dark."

Alex grinned, looking at her as if getting lost might not be such a bad idea. He led Stacy into the trees, following a rocky path. There wasn't anything to see as they walked, except trees that cast eerie shadows in the moonlight. There wasn't room to walk side by side, so Stacy stumbled awkwardly after Alex in her high-heeled snakeskin boots and tight designer jeans. After a while, they came to a grassy clearing with a fallen tree. Alex sat down against the tree.

"Come here," he slurred, gesturing to Stacy.

"But there might be bugs," Stacy objected. "I can't see anything."

Alex grasped her hand and tugged her down to the ground, spilling the beer he had carried with him. "Who cares?" He pulled her roughly against him. "I've been wanting to do this all night. Ever since I saw you in those tight jeans." He kissed her, hard.

After the first jolt of surprise, Stacy began to

enjoy the kiss, knowing that a guy any of the APA's would gladly date wanted to be with her. She kissed him back, her arms going around his neck, her hands in his dark brown hair, liking the feel of his strong arms tight around her.

"Hey, that's nice," he murmured. "Ve-ry nice." His lips moved against her throat, and she could smell the sharp, woodsy scent of his after-shave. She pressed closer. "Mmm," he said into her ear, "I *like* the way you move."

He kissed her again, his breath coming harder, and Stacy began to tremble. She sighed and let herself lean against him as he touched her eyelashes and her cheek with his fingers, then her throat. Then his hand dipped to the front of her blouse.

Stacy pulled back slightly from the warm pressure of Alex's fingers. She'd let her suitemates think she was experienced, with all those stories about guys, but they were just that—stories. She'd come close a couple of times, but she'd always chickened out. And she didn't want her first time to be out in the woods, with someone she barely knew.

"Alex, don't," she whispered, pulling his hand away.

"What?" he asked in a muffled voice. His fingers were more urgent now, feeling for the pearl-cover snaps on her shirt. "Mmm," he said. "You really turn me on."

"Don't," she said sharply.

His fingers pressed harder, and he found the first snap and pulled it open. She pushed his hand away and struggled to sit up. "I didn't come here to . . . that's not . . . I mean, I *really* don't want to."

He dropped his hand to her stomach and began to kiss her again. "It's okay, babe," he murmured huskily, his hand moving lower. "Just relax. I know it takes some girls longer to get going."

Suddenly Stacy felt cold. "I'm not *going* anywhere," she said, pulling away from him, "except back to the party. Now." She sat up and snapped the front of her blouse together.

"Hey," he demanded, "what's your problem? Why are you so uptight?"

"I'm not uptight," Stacy replied. "I just don't want to, that's all."

Frowning, Alex sat back against the tree, folding his arms across his chest. "What's the deal? The way you were coming on, I had no idea you were just a tease."

"I wasn't coming on," Stacy said between clenched teeth.

"Oh, yeah?" he growled. "Listen, Little Miss Innocence, you were coming on to me plenty at the Alpha party when we danced together. You were coming on to me just now when you kissed me." He scowled darkly. "Either that, or you were doing a pretty good job faking it."

Stacy stood up.

"Where do you think you're going?" he demanded.

"Back to the party," she said, starting off.

He scrambled to his feet. "Well, you're going the wrong way," he said. "The party's over there."

"No, it isn't," Stacy said, "it's *that* way."

Alex shook his head and strode to the edge of the clearing. "Are you coming?"

After five minutes of stumbling, Stacy knew they were lost. The moon wasn't bright enough to light their way, and the trail had disappeared into a steep ravine, filled with deadfalls. Stacy's boots were killing her feet. She had already slipped and ripped the knee of her jeans. This was starting to look like a really bad night. When they gave up on the trail and tried to retrace their path, they couldn't even find the clearing.

"Damn," Alex said, sitting down on a rock. He glowered at her. "A hell of a way to spend an evening."

"We should have gone the other—" Stacy stopped and bit her lip. There was no point in reminding him that it was his fault they were lost. She sat down on a log, wishing they'd eaten something before they left the party. She was so hungry she felt dizzy. And to make matters worse, her left ankle throbbed painfully. She must have twisted it somehow.

"Yeah, I know," Alex growled. "But we *didn't* go the other way, so we're stuck. Maybe we'll be here all night." He laughed. "Wouldn't *that* be a kick? Stuck all night in the woods with a virgin?"

Stacy turned away, the tears welling behind her eyelids.

"Hey!" Alex said, looking around. "What's that?"

Stacy raised her head, listening, too. Not far

away she could hear a truck, and music, too. "Over there." She pointed eagerly. "It's coming from that direction."

Alex stood up. "Well, we can't get any *more* lost," he said. "Come on."

With Stacy limping painfully, they started scrambling down a steep slope through dense underbrush. A long branch jabbed Stacy's cheek just under her left eye, and she tore her right sleeve on another branch. Just when she thought she was going to give up and collapse, they came to a gravel road, just in time to hail the old Ford that was pulling a hay wagon.

Nancy peered over a bale of hay from the top of the wagon. Beside her, somebody turned down a portable stereo, and a dozen curious faces looked down. "God, Stacy," Nancy said, "what happened to *you*? You're a mess!"

Stacy glanced down at herself. The sleeve of her plaid shirt was torn nearly off, there was a huge rip in the knee of her jeans, and her hands were scratched and bloody. She tried to smile, but her lips trembled.

"Oh, it's nothing," she said. "Just a few scratches, that's all."

Brenda's head popped over another bale. "It's not just a few scratches," she said suggestively, eyeing Alex. "Really, Stacy, you look like you've spent the evening rolling around in the bushes."

For a minute, Stacy stared at her angrily. Then suddenly she couldn't take it anymore; she started crying. She didn't care who saw her or what she looked like. So many rotten things had happened lately—everything since coming to Hawthorne had gone wrong. Was anything ever going to go her way again?

Chapter 8

"No," Stacy moaned. Someone was shaking her shoulder. "No, leave me alone. Please leave me alone." She pulled the pillow over her head.

"Stacy, come on, wake up."

"What?" Stacy mumbled. "What? Who?" She pulled the covers up around her neck. "What time is it?"

"It's nearly ten," Terry said, sitting on the edge of the bed. "I know you got in late last night, but we've decided to go to Atlanta today, and we want . . ."

Stacy dove under the pillow. Last night? The cookout. Alex. Riding back in the wagon, with everybody trying not to upset her or look at her. Sandy driving the Mercedes back to campus because Stacy's ankle was sprained. Alex nowhere to be seen. And the worst—Brenda asking, in a dying-ofcuriosity whisper that everybody must have heard, "Is it true that he *raped* her?"

"What's the matter?" Roni asked, coming into the bedroom. "Hangover?"

"Oh, God," Stacy groaned, and rolled over. Every bone in her body ached, and she felt feverish.

"Listen," said Terry, "we wouldn't be trying to wake you up, but we want you to come with us to Atlanta." She leaned forward, her voice cajoling. "We're going to Neiman's."

"No, I don't want to," Stacy said, grabbing for the pillow again. There was a disgruntled *meow*, and Stacy opened one eye. Bandit was sitting on the pillow watching her. "I don't want to go anywhere," she said, turning over on her back with enormous effort. "I feel like staying in bed."

"Wow," Terry said. "What in the world happened to your eye?"

"My eye?" Stacy propped herself up painfully on one elbow. "What about my eye?"

Roni handed Sam's mirror to Stacy. "Better take a deep breath before you look at yourself," she advised.

Stacy looked into the mirror. "Oh, Lord," she said.

"It looks like you got in a fight," Terry said, touching Stacy's temple gingerly with her finger. "It's pretty bruised. I'll get you a warm washcloth."

"How did it happen?" asked Roni. "It wasn't that guy Alex, was it?"

"No, it wasn't Alex," Stacy said in a defensive tone. "I got poked in the eye with a branch or something, that's all." She lay back on the pillow, shutting her eyes.

"A branch?" Roni asked. "It looks like somebody *hit* you."

Terry came back with the cloth. "Who would do that?"

"Nobody *hit* me," Stacy said wearily, pressing the warm cloth to her tender eye. "We got lost in the woods, and I fell down a hill, that's all."

"It looks like it'll be black and blue for a couple of days," Terry said. "It's probably a good idea for you to stay in bed."

"But I have to go to the bathroom," Stacy said. She sat up. "Thank God it's the weekend. At least I don't have to go to class." Stacy stood up—and then sat down again. "Ooh, my ankle!"

At that moment, Sam came into the room, wearing her jogging clothes. "Well, I'm back," she said. "I'll get changed, and we can leave for Atlanta whenever Stacy is—"

She stopped suddenly, peering at Stacy. "God, Stacy," she exclaimed, "you're a mess! Were you in a wreck or something?"

"No, it wasn't a wreck," Stacy said, lifting her leg back onto the bed. "I fell down a hill in the dark. I knew I twisted my ankle, but I didn't think it was this bad." She pulled up her pajama leg and looked at her ankle: it was puffy and blue, and it hurt a lot.

Terry probed it with her fingers. "I think you've got a fracture," she told Stacy. "Let's go over to the infirmary and get it X-rayed."

"That's what we get for rooming with a premed," Roni told Sam. "Instant diagnoses."

Stacy looked up at Terry, dismayed. "A fracture?" she said, thinking of the homework she'd planned to catch up on this weekend. "I don't have time!"

Terry picked up Stacy's jeans. "Do you want to put these on, or would you rather go in pajamas?"

"I don't think she ought to wear jeans," Sam objected. "Sweatpants would be looser." She went to the drawer as Terry left the room. "Here are mine."

"But I'm not going to the infirmary," Stacy said. "All I need is a little rest and—"

"Oh, yes, you *are* going to the infirmary," Roni told her firmly. "Here. Put these on."

"But I don't *want* to," Stacy whined.

"Frankly," Sam said as she pulled Stacy up and gave her a sweatshirt, "it doesn't matter *what* you want. Dr. Conklin says you might have a fracture, so you're going to the infirmary to get X-rayed. It'll mess up everybody's year if you die in our suite."

Terry came back with a pair of moccasins and slipped them on Stacy's feet. She looked around. "I wish we had something to use for a crutch. You shouldn't be putting any weight on that ankle."

"Hey, wait a minute," said Roni. "She's not going to *walk* to the infirmary, is she? It's too far away."

"Well, if I can't walk, I can't go," Stacy said.

"Oh, shut up," Roni said. "I've got an idea. We can take your car."

"Yes, that's a good idea," Terry agreed. She put her hand on Stacy's forehead. "I think she might even

have a little temperature. She looks awfully pale."
She frowned at Stacy. "When did you eat last?"

Eat? Stacy tried to think. Everything was a little
fuzzy.

"Stacy," Terry said again, "when did you eat
last?"

"Eat last?" Stacy repeated, remembering that she
hadn't eaten anything at the party, and she'd skipped
lunch, too. "Oh, I don't know. Breakfast yesterday,
maybe. I think I had yogurt."

"Friday morning?" Terry exclaimed. "You can't
go for twenty-four hours on one container of yogurt,
Stacy."

Sam picked up Stacy's bag and fished out her
keys. "Let's go," she said.

Roni took Stacy's hand. "Come on, Stace."

Stacy stood up and put her foot down gingerly.
"See?" she said. "See, I can walk on . . . ooh!" She
swayed dizzily and clutched at Toni, the pain in her
ankle shooting up through her entire leg.

"You take one side," Sam instructed Roni, "I'll
take the other. Terry, you go to Pam's room and get
the key to the elevator. Tell her Stacy's hurt and can't
use the stairs." And before she knew it, Stacy was
being gently carried along to the elevator.

"What happened? Is she badly hurt?" Pam asked,
rushing up with Terry, the elevator key in her hand.
She looked at Stacy. "What happened to your *eye*?"

"A branch," Stacy told her, wishing that people
would stop making such a fuss over one bruise. "I got
hit in the eye by a branch. It was an accident."

Pam unlocked the elevator. "Wow—I hope you're okay," she said as the elevator door opened.

"Listen, Stacy, are you sure you're not covering for Alex?" Roni asked.

"Alex?" Pam asked. "Who's Alex?"

"The guy she was out with when this happened," Terry explained.

"Listen, you guys, you've *got* to believe me," Stacy said. "It *wasn't* Alex. He was a huge jerk, but he didn't attack me. I wouldn't protect this guy." She leaned weakly against the wall. All this commotion was making her feel sick. The elevator rumbled to a jarring stop, and the door opened onto the first-floor hallway.

"I'll go get the car," Terry volunteered. She scurried off with Stacy's keys, her wheat-blond hair flying.

"Okay, Stace," Sam said gently, "here we go." She put her arm around Stacy's waist. "Just lean on me."

"Let me help, too," Pam said, coming to the other side.

"I'm perfectly all right," Stacy said. "I can walk to the car by myself." She took a tentative step and gasped, swaying against Sam. "Well, maybe not."

"Oh, hi, y'all," said a cheerful voice. "What's going on? Where's everybody going?"

Stacy groaned and covered her eyes with her hands. It was Brenda.

"For pity's sake," Brenda said in a horrified tone, "just look at you!" She turned to Pam. "She looked bad enough last night when we picked her and Alex up on that dirt road. But she looks much worse this morning." She shook her head. "Much worse."

"She'll be all right soon," Sam said soothingly. "We're going to the infirmary."

"I told everybody that she should go last night," Brenda said. "When there's an attack, you ought to get a doctor's exam right away so that—"

"But there *wasn't* any attack!" Stacy cried. "We fell down a hill. It was an accident."

Brenda looked at her pityingly. "That's what she said last night, too. But we were all there, and we could see. Why, Alex didn't have a scratch on him."

"Listen, Sam," Stacy said dizzily over the roaring in her ears, "I really think I'd better sit down somewhere."

Sam tightened her arm around Stacy's waist and began to steer her gently down the hall. "It's only a dozen more steps," she said. "Can you make it?"

Stacy nodded weakly. "I think so."

"I'd better know *exactly* what happened last night," Pam was saying as she and Roni walked with Brenda behind Stacy and Sam.

Brenda lowered her voice. "Nobody really knows for sure," she said, "because Stacy won't tell. But I know what everybody *thinks*."

"What's that?" asked Roni. "What does everybody think?"

Brenda cleared her throat. "Everybody thinks," she said in a loud whisper, "that Alex raped her."

It was the last thing Stacy heard before she fainted into Sam's arms.

Chapter 9

The doctor came into the examining room and smiled at Stacy. "Hi," she said casually. "I'm Dr. Emerson. Feeling better?"

Stacy nodded mutely.

Dr. Emerson went to the lighted wall frame that held the X-rays of Stacy's ankle. "I don't see any sign of a fracture," she said, studying the X-ray. "The ankle's sprained, though, and you're going to have to stay off it completely this weekend—and use crutches for a week or so."

Stacy breathed a sigh of relief. "Then I can go back to the dorm."

"Not so fast," replied the doctor. She picked up a chart on a clipboard and looked at it. "Your RA tells me that there's a question about how all this happened." She looked up from the chart, her eyes direct. "I have to ask you this, Stacy. Were you raped last night?"

Stacy shook her head. "No," she whispered. "It was bad, but not *that* bad. I fell down a hill, that's all."

Dr. Emerson picked up Stacy's wrist and began to take her pulse. "Do you know what date rape or acquaintance rape is?"

"I think so," Stacy said.

There was a pause. "It's when somebody you're going out with or someone you know as a friend forces you to have sex with him," Dr. Emerson said, making a note on the chart. "Often, the girl is afraid to talk about it. She thinks that no one will believe that it really *was* rape. Or she feels it's *her* fault for leading him on." She began to examine Stacy's scratched eye. "As a matter of fact," she added, "we usually find out that the guys are repeat offenders. If one girl would tell, we might be able to keep one of her friends from getting into the same fix. So if anything happened, Stacy, you're not doing anyone a favor by covering it up."

"Alex *did* make a pass at me," Stacy said in a low voice. "But nothing happened. I mean, he quit when I asked him to. And then we got lost, and I fell down a hill." She could feel the tears trickling from the corners of her eyes. "Brenda—a girl who was on the wagon—keeps saying that . . . that it happened. But it didn't."

The doctor looked at her. "You're sure?"

"I'm sure."

"Well, then," Dr. Emerson said briskly, "there's

only one more thing we need to talk about." She put down the chart. "Your friends tell me you're not eating well. Are you dieting?"

Stacy couldn't believe her suitemates had been talking about her again. "I try to keep my weight down," she admitted. "I don't like to be fat."

"Tell me what you normally eat in a day," Doctor Emerson said, her voice warm and encouraging.

"Some yogurt," Stacy said. "Raw vegetables, stuff like that."

"Diet pills?"

Stacy looked down and didn't answer.

The doctor looked at her. "Look, Stacy, you fainted this morning. Fainting is a danger sign that you need to take seriously. It says that your system has had just about all it can take, that it's going to check out temporarily." She put her hand on Stacy's arm. "Your friends say that you haven't eaten for a couple of days. Do you know what a fast of that length can do to your system?"

"I suppose," Stacy said in a low voice, "that it could make you weak, slow down your blood or something."

"You suppose right." Dr. Emerson sat down on the corner of her desk. "It can actually dump toxic wastes into your bloodstream. And if you've got some vitamin deficiencies, you could be in for some real trouble." She began to write something on a piece of paper. "I want to see you stop fasting and gain back some of that weight."

"But I don't want to gain," Stacy said. "I need to

lose five more pounds, and then I'll be exactly where I want to be."

"Stacy, your weight is *fine* now. In fact, you're a little on the light side for your height and frame. Dr. Emerson held out a prescription blank on which she'd written a name. "Last year, we started a program for people with eating disorders. Here's the phone number of the woman who helps organize things. Why don't you give her a call?"

Reluctantly, Stacy took the paper. "But I don't *have* an eating disorder," she protested. "And anyway, I've got a lot to do. I don't have time for—"

"Then make time." Dr. Emerson went to the door. "You can get off the crutches on Friday. But right how, I want you to go get something to eat. Something substantial, not just yogurt. Okay?"

"Okay," Stacy agreed. Dr. Emerson was being pretty nice, and she had to admit that she really *was* hungry. Or was it famished?

"What did the doctor say?" Terry asked, getting up out of the waiting room seat and hurrying over to Stacy.

"She said to stay off it for a couple of days," Stacy said, leaning on the crutches the nurse had given her.

"And what did she say about your fainting?" asked Sam.

"Oh, that," Stacy said evasively as they started out of the waiting room, "was because of the pain." She put on a grin. "You'd faint, too, if you were standing around on a sprained ankle."

"Did you talk to her about Alex?" Roni asked as she held the door open.

Stacy frowned. "Roni, that stuff about Alex— that's just Brenda's vivid imagination. You know how she is. Alex . . . well, he *did* make a pass, but he stopped when I asked him to."

"Well, then, I guess we've got a different kind of problem," Pam said. "A different person, anyway."

"Right," Terry agreed. "Her name is Brenda."

"Well, I vote that we don't try to resolve everything now," Sam said eagerly. "This vision of blueberry waffles with maple syrup and creamery butter keeps dancing in my head. Who wants to go to Pancakes Plus with me?"

Stacy smiled. "I'd love to go. Even on crutches."

Later, back in their suite, the girls insisted that Stacy lie down on the sofa, with pillows from their beds under her back and Sam's crocheted afghan over her. Roni volunteered to go to the library to get the books Stacy needed for her English paper, Sam gave Stacy her notes for the art history lectures she had missed, and Terry, domestic as always, made hot chocolate.

"I don't *want* any hot chocolate," Stacy protested, thinking of all the calories she'd just consumed. But when Terry looked hurt, she gave in and had some. Then she felt so full that she fell asleep over Sam's notes, with Bandit lying on her chest. She didn't wake up until the middle of the afternoon, when the phone rang. It was for Terry.

"Who was that?" Stacy asked curiously after Terry hung up, looking pleased.

"Oh, just someone from biology lab," said Terry. "A guy named Brian."

Stacy raised her eyebrows. Terry was blushing. "Brian?" she asked. "Is he somebody you like?"

"Well, not *like*, actually," Terry said. "I mean, as in boyfriend. He's a nice guy and all that, but I'm not interested."

"Oh?" asked Stacy. Bandit put up his head, and she scratched his ears. "Why not?"

"Well, you know," Terry said. She picked up the chemistry book she'd been studying. "There's just no time. What with studying and working in the costume shop and stuff like that." Terry had a work-study job with the theater department.

"Mmm," said Stacy. "Well, if you had more time, would you go out with him?"

Terry considered. "I might," she said. "If I had more time. But I don't." She pointed to the stack of books on the coffee table. "If you need more books," she said, "I'm going to the lab to meet Brian in a little while, and I'll be glad to get them."

"Oh, I see," Stacy remarked, "you *have* got a date. A study date."

"No, not really," Terry said, going back to her book. "I mean, we're studying together, but it's not a date."

Stacy gave up with a smile and began to sort through Sam's lecture notes. On her lap, Bandit stretched, then scooted playfully across the back of the sofa, where he dug in his claws and began to scratch.

At that moment there was a knock on the door, and Pam stuck her head in. "How are you doing?" she asked.

Hastily, Stacy grabbed Bandit and shoved him under the afghan, busying herself with Sam's lecture notes. "Oh, I'm fine," she said, glancing up. "Just fine." Her heart began to beat double time. If Pam discovered Bandit, she might throw him out of the dorm. Where would he go? What would he eat? Whom would *she* hug?

Pam came into the room and looked at the books Roni had brought and the empty chocolate mug. "It looks like you're taken care of," she said, sitting down on the edge of the coffee table. "I'm on my way to the drugstore. Is there anything you want? Aspirin or anything?"

Stacy shook her head. Under the afghan, Bandit was beginning to squirm. "No, nothing," she said, trying to act casual. "I don't need anything." Bandit squirmed harder, and she flattened her leg on him to hold him down.

"You're sure? Candy, notebook paper? A paperback novel, maybe?" Pam looked down. "That's interesting," she remarked, pointing. "Which one of you drinks milk from a saucer?"

Stacy looked. Sure enough, there was a half-empty saucer of milk. Maybe Terry had fed Bandit while she was asleep. "Oh, that," she said, thinking quickly. "That's just one of Sam's little experiments."

"Experiments?" Pam stared at the saucer. "What's she experimenting with?"

"Oh, you know, for political science," Stacy said. "Something like a follow-up to eating rice for a week. They're always doing crazy things in Lewis's political science class."

Pam frowned. "Well, tell her that she shouldn't leave food around. You know the problem we've got in this dorm with cockroaches and mice." She stood up, shaking her head. "What we need is a good *cat*. One that's really enthusiastic about hunting mice. I found one in my shoe this morning."

"Which?" Terry asked, trying to distract Pam's attention from the saucer. "A cat or a mouse?"

"Hey, fun-ny," Pam said with deep sarcasm.

Terry grinned. "Did it bite?"

"Listen," Pam said, "it wouldn't be funny to you if you stepped on a mouse barefoot."

Stacy put both hands under the afghan and grabbed Bandit, who had squirmed free and was trying to wriggle out. Bandit twisted and writhed, mewing quietly but plaintively. Across the room Terry was watching; her face getting redder and redder as she tried not to laugh.

"If you don't mind," Stacy said with an enormous yawn, "I think I'd better have a nap." If she pretended to fall asleep, maybe Pam would leave.

Pam looked at Terry, who was still trying to swallow a giggle. "I just don't understand, Terry, why stepping on a mouse is so funny."

"Oh, it's not the mouse," Terry said in a strangled voice. "It's something"—she coughed—"in my . . . in my book. Something funny."

"Something funny in that chemistry book?" Pam asked, looking puzzled. "Then they must have changed organic since I suffered through it."

"They must have," she agreed with a smothered hiccup. "Or maybe it's all in your attitude. I mean, some people think some things are funny." She hiccuped again. "Some people don't."

Pam opened the door. "You'd better take the rest of the afternoon off, Terry," she advised. "The strain of studying's finally getting to you." Then she was gone.

Bandit wriggled out from under the afghan and fell off the sofa, doing a somersault in midair, while Stacy and Terry collapsed into giggles.

"Maybe we could sell shares in Bandit," Stacy gasped helplessly after a few minutes. "You know, rent him to other suites to keep mice out of people's shoes."

"Kitty patrol," Terry agreed, and they both broke up completely. It was the best laugh Stacy had had in a long time. It almost made her forget about what had happened with Alex, and about Brenda and her stories. Almost—but not quite. Her stomach knotted at the thought of those two. Sooner or later, she was going to have to get off the couch and face them —and everyone else who knew about her humiliating night.

After a while, Terry left for the lab. Stacy pulled the covers up over her head and fell into a fitful sleep.

* * *

It was much later that night when the call came from Stacy's father. She was in bed, with her ankle propped up on a pillow, rewriting her English paper.

"Hi, Stace," her father said in his deep, resonant voice. "How's my favorite girl?"

"Oh, hi, Jason," Stacy said, delighted. "How's the election coming?"

Her father tried to laugh, but he sounded very tired. "Harder and faster," he said. "You know the routine—lots of hand-shaking, personal appearances, news conferences. And the newspapers have it in for me, as usual. But it'll all be over soon," he added. "I'll tell you about it when I see you next weekend."

"Next weekend!" Stacy exclaimed. "But what—"

"I'm coming to Atlanta on Friday," Jason said.

"That's wonderful! Can you come up to Hawthorne? Listen, there's a football game that afternoon. We can go with my roommates."

"Or maybe you could drive to Atlanta for the day," Jason suggested.

"I'd rather have you come here," Stacy said. "I want you to meet everybody—my roommates, my sorority sisters. Guess what! I'm running for executive council in Alpha Pi!"

"Hey, how about that?" His laugh sounded a little strained. "And you want me to help you with your campaign?"

"Yeah, well, you could, you know," Stacy said. "There's a pledge meeting on Saturday morning, a meet-the-candidates sort of thing. I could introduce you." Having a state senator for a father certainly couldn't hurt her chances.

"Sure," he said, "if that's what you want. Well, okay then, see you Saturday."

Right after they'd hung up, Stacy realized that she'd forgotten to ask about Thanksgiving.

Chapter 10

On Monday, Stacy woke to pouring rain. It was definitely a bad omen. Her eye was still a garish purple that makeup only accentuated, and her ankle was throbbing. How was she going to manage crutches in the rain? What had Brenda been saying about her all weekend? And Alex—what had *he* been telling people?

When she finally made it to the dining hall, Stacy shucked the poncho she'd borrowed from Terry. She hesitated in front of the serving line, remembering what Dr. Emerson had said about eating. She shouldn't feel guilty for following the doctor's orders, should she? Maybe she could have something more than yogurt while she was recuperating. She peered longingly at the scrambled eggs. No, she'd had a huge meal on Saturday, she'd snacked Sunday, and she'd spent both days on the couch. Besides, a regu-

lar tray of food would be too difficult to handle. She
turned toward the cooler to get the usual.

"Hey, what happened to you?"

Stacy looked up and felt her face go red and her
heart beat quicker. It was Pete Young. His curly red
hair was beaded with raindrops, and he was smiling
down at her, his eyes curious.

"Looks like you met a freight train in the dark," he
drawled. "You okay?"

"I'm okay," Stacy said. She shifted awkwardly on
her crutches. "My ankle's just sprained, that's all,
and I've got a few bruises. Nothing serious."

"Good." Pete took the tray out from under her
arm and nodded toward the eggs. "Scrambled?
Poached? Fried?"

"Thanks," Stacy said, "but I'm having yogurt. It's
easier to manage."

"That's okay," Pete said. "I can carry your tray
—no problem. What's your pleasure?"

"But I don't want—"

"Listen, handling those crutches in that rain is
going to take a lot of energy," Pete said firmly.
"Scrambled or fried?"

"But really, I'd rather . . ." Stacy sputtered.

"Didn't your mother ever tell you," Pete said,
cocking one eyebrow, "that you ought to start with a
good breakfast?" He ordered scrambled eggs. "I
guess she didn't," he said with an appraising glance
at Stacy. "You look as if you haven't had a good
breakfast in months. Do you usually skip breakfast?
Sleep late?"

"Do you always ask personal questions?" Stacy

demanded. "No, I *don't* sleep late. I'm usually up and jogging by six-thirty."

"Well, that's good," he said. "Exercise is good for you. Just like eating. Bacon or sausage?"

Stacy looked at him. His blue-green eyes were intent on hers, his face serious. He had high cheekbones, she noticed. Not bad for a boy from Hawthorne Springs.

"Look, do you really think you can just barge in and tell me what to—"

"Bacon or sausage?"

"Bacon," she said with a resigned sigh. Really. This Pete Young was too much. No guy had ever had the nerve to tell her what to do before. Most guys waited for Stacy Swanson's wish to be *their* command.

"One bacon, one sausage, please," he ordered, "and two bowls of grits. With gravy."

Stacy shuddered. That was going *too* far. "I don't want grits," she protested. "Or gravy, either." Grits and gravy? How fattening. And how *southern*. If Sydney could see her now, she'd absolutely die.

"Then I'll eat yours," Pete said, putting both bowls on the tray. He picked up the tray and started for the drink dispensers. "Milk?"

"Coffee, please."

"Milk's better for you, you know." Stacy smiled back at him. "But if you insist," he said, sticking a cup under the coffee spigot. "I don't know how you can drink this stuff." He carried the loaded tray to the cash register. Stacy reached for her meal ticket in the backpack Sam had lent to her, but Pete put up his hand. "I talked you into breakfast," he said with a grin, "I pay for it." He motioned with his head. "Come on."

Stacy looked around. What would her sorority sisters think if they saw her eating with a townie? But she didn't see anybody from Alpha Pi, so she followed him to a table beside the window. Outside, the lake was gray and pockmarked with rain. The pine trees bent with the wind, and brown leaves flew by in flurries. Stacy shivered as she pulled Sam's backpack off.

"It looks cold," she said, cautiously tasting her scrambled eggs. They were hot and delicious, and she took a bigger bite. "Almost like up north."

"Sometimes it even snows," Pete said with a nod, dumping ketchup onto his scrambled eggs.

"It snows? In Georgia?" Stacy stared at him in disbelief. "And you eat ketchup on eggs in Georgia, too?"

"Sure." He pulled his bowl of grits and gravy toward him. The grits looked like a bad version of cream of wheat to Stacy.

"Try some? LuAnn's southern cooking at its finest." LuAnn was the chief cook of the Commons dining hall: she made the best school food, everybody said, in the whole South.

Stacy shook her head. The gravy actually smelled heavenly, but it was probably swimming with calories. "No, thanks," she said. "The bacon and eggs are enough."

He looked out the window. "Yeah, we'll probably get some snow this winter," he said. "Last year, just before Thanksgiving, we got two inches. Enough for sledding on the hill behind Merrill Hall." He glanced back at her. "Get your pottery project done?"

"No," she said, "I have to glaze the mugs today."

"So," he said. Stacy noticed that there were crow's-feet at the corners of his eyes. "Maybe I'll see you at the studio this afternoon, huh?"

Stacy looked up at the clock. "Oops! I've got to go," she said hurriedly, pushing her plate away. "I'm going to be late to English." She picked up Sam's backpack to swing it onto her shoulders.

Pete stood up. "I'll take that," he said, lifting it out of her hands. He picked up the crutches that were leaning against the wall beside her seat and handed them to her.

"But I have to go all the way over to the English building," Stacy protested.

"So? My sociology class is in Baines. The last time I looked, the two buildings were right next door. Anyway, the sidewalks are crowded. You need somebody to run interference for you." He held out his hand. "Ready?"

Stacy shook her head. "You don't take no for an answer, do you?"

Pete grinned.

As they ducked through the rain to the English building, Stacy learned that Pete was a sophomore, that his father and mother ran a small grocery store in Hawthorne Springs, that he had six brothers and sisters, and that he planned to transfer to Georgia Tech next year so he could study engineering.

"Isn't that something you're supposed to start in

your freshman year?" Stacy asked, out of breath. They were climbing the stone steps to the English building. The rain had slacked up, but managing her crutches in the nine o'clock traffic jam was a lot harder than she had expected; she was glad Pete was carrying her bookbag.

Pete nodded. "Yeah, Hawthorne's strictly liberal arts—no engineering. But I wanted to spend a year here, so I could be close to home." He grinned. "I also wanted to learn something about history and literature before I started cramming all those numbers and formulas into my head. Who knows? Maybe I won't want to be an engineer." He opened the front door. "Managing okay?"

"Yeah, thanks." Dr. Marshall's classroom was on the first floor, so she didn't need to climb more stairs. She pulled her dripping poncho off and tried to fluff her damp hair.

Pete looked at her and grinned. "You look like a little kid with your hair wet," he said. "A little kid with a big black eye."

Stacy made a face. "I must look pretty awful."

"Just pretty," Pete replied, his eyes on hers.

Stacy blushed. This guy—he couldn't be for real. She'd never met anybody who said such outrageously direct things. She took her bookbag. "Well, uh, thanks for carrying my books. Saying that really makes me *feel* like a little kid."

Pete grinned. "Where's your next class?"

"Music. It's in Fine Arts. But you don't need to . . ."

He turned to go down the stairs. "It's on my way."

He looked up at her, one hand on the banister. "Hey, maybe I'd better have something to call you."

"Oh," she said. After he'd bought her breakfast and carried her books, she couldn't believe she still hadn't told him her name. "Well, you might try Stacy."

"Stacy. I like that. I suppose there's something else that goes with it? Like a last name?"

Stacy smiled. "Yeah," she said. "Swanson."

"Okay, Stacy Swanson. See you in an hour," he called, and clattered out the door.

Dr. Marshall was discussing *Antony and Cleopatra*, a play Stacy liked because she had seen it in New York. But she found it hard to focus her attention. For one thing, she was still embarrassed over her silly stunt last week, and she had to avoid looking at Dr. Marshall. For another, her thoughts kept wandering to Pete Young, which was utterly ridiculous. After all, she'd only let Pete help because he'd insisted on it. She hadn't changed her mind about him. But she had to smile when she thought of the way he'd taken charge of breakfast. It was nice to have somebody make a fuss over her—especially on a day when she felt so down about her ankle, and Alex, and Brenda. Actually, when she thought about it, she couldn't really remember *anyone* ever taking such good care of her—except for her suitemates, this weekend. It felt good to have friends, but Stacy wasn't used to it yet. She felt uncomfortable about depending on other people. Usually she just relied on herself—and her parents' money. She wasn't sure she liked this new vulnerability thing.

"Hey, what'd you do to your face? You look awful." Stacy cringed. It was Roger, standing beside her desk, looking horrified.

Stacy pulled her poncho over her head and put her copy of the play in her bookbag. "A little accident," she said, picking up her crutches.

"Looks like somebody gave you the old one-two right in the eye," Roger said. "How does the other guy look?"

"Ready to brave the elements?" Pete interrupted, walking up to Stacy and brandishing a dripping umbrella with a bent rib.

"Where'd you get the umbrella?" Stacy asked, surprised and grateful for an excuse to get away from Roger.

"Lost and found, over in Baines," Pete said. "It's a monsoon out there."

Roger frowned at Pete. "Look, I'll call you," he told Stacy. "Okay?"

"Okay." Stacy shrugged and hobbled after Pete.

Pete opened the umbrella just inside the door and turned to Stacy. "Is that guy somebody you go out with?" he asked.

"No," she said, "just somebody from class." She peered up at the sky. "Wow, it's really pouring." The water was coming down in sheets, and the sidewalk was ankle deep.

"You ready to make like a duck?" Pete asked.

Stacy nodded. "I guess so," she said, pulling up the hood of Terry's poncho. She laughed ruefully.

"Quack, quack." They went out into the storm, both laughing.

The rest of the day, Pete helped Stacy get to her classes, carrying her books and the umbrella, holding doors open, helping her up stairs. Since it was still raining the next day, too, it seemed natural for him to appear at the door first thing in the morning. She introduced him to Terry and Roni, and they talked for a few minutes. On Wednesday morning, he joked that picking her up might get to be a habit. On Thursday, Terry asked Stacy about him.

"He just wants to help while I'm on these stupid crutches," Stacy said. She yanked her shoelace, breaking it. "God," she muttered, "I'll be so glad when I can wear *clothes* again. I'm getting tired of sneakers and jeans."

"He's really nice, Stacy," Terry said. "And he's nice-looking, too." Stacy thought she sounded envious. "Has he asked you out?"

Stacy retied her lace. "No, but I wouldn't go out with him anyway," she said. "He's a townie."

Terry looked surprised. "So?"

"So we don't have a lot in common," Stacy said as she combed her hair. "He's not anywhere near my type."

Terry looked at her reflectively. "Well," she said, "he's a nice guy, and I'd hate to see him, well, hurt."

Stacy put down her comb and glanced at Terry. "So what makes you think he's going to get hurt?" she asked.

Terry shrugged. "Don't you think he likes you?"

"Well, maybe. But I let him know I wasn't interested in anything romantic from the beginning."

"Yeah?" Terry asked. "Are you sure you were telling the truth?"

Stacy stared at her. "Terry, one day someone who doesn't appreciate your other qualities is going to give *you* a black eye for being such a nag."

"You didn't answer my question," Terry said as Pete's familiar knock sounded on the suite door.

On Thursday night, Stacy was reviewing her art history notes at her desk, wearing her pink pajamas and robe, with Bandit asleep on her English book. Just before nine, Nancy Greer came by.

"I just wanted to remind you," Nancy said, unzipping her red jacket and sitting down on the bed, "about the meeting on Saturday morning." She looked at Stacy's ankle, which was still wrapped in an Ace bandage. "Are you still planning on running?"

"Of course," Stacy replied. She put down her pencil, and Bandit stretched and yawned. "In fact, my father's going to be here. It's okay if I bring him along, isn't it?"

"Sure, Nancy said. "We'd love to have him." She glanced at Bandit. "I thought they wouldn't let you keep pets in the dorm."

Stacy grinned and picked Bandit up. "What they don't know won't hurt them." It was getting to be her standard line.

Nancy nodded. "Yeah, I suppose so," she said. She hesitated. "Uh, how's your ankle? I heard you've been on crutches all week."

"Yes." Stacy sighed. "But it's just sprained. Tomorrow I can get off the crutches and everything will be back to normal." She grinned. "I'm really looking forward to the election. I think . . . well, I really think I could do a good job."

Nancy paused. "Uh, Stacy, there's another reason I came over." She shifted uncomfortably. "I, uh, well, there's a rumor going around that you ought to know about. That is, if you haven't heard it already."

Stacy felt a chill in the room and pulled her robe tighter around her. "A rumor? What kind of rumor?"

"Actually," Nancy said, frowning, "it's about you and Alex. About what happened last Friday night."

"But nothing happened," Stacy protested. "I mean, other than me twisting my ankle and getting scratched up when I fell down the hill."

Nancy looked at her closely. "*I* believe you," she said. Bandit had climbed to the edge of the desk, and she reached over and rubbed his ears. "But some of the girls have been listening to Brenda, and they think you're covering up. They're saying that you should turn Alex in, instead of letting him get away with it."

"But they're just gossiping," Stacy said anxiously. "Doesn't anybody *see* that? Nothing happened! I can't turn in somebody who didn't do anything!"

"Some people probably realize that it's all just nasty rumors, but unfortunately they're not the ones who are doing the talking. And Alex . . . well, he seems to be encouraging the gossip." Nancy glanced up. "Maybe it's a kind of macho thing. Maybe he likes people to think he's some kind of bigtime operator."

"God," Stacy whispered, "this whole thing is just disgusting." She swallowed hard. "What can I do, Nancy?"

"Well, I'll do what *I* can to set people straight. I can't really think of anything that *you* can do. Except..." Nancy's mouth tightened. "Stacy, I hate to say this, but maybe this isn't the time for you to run for executive council. I mean, the election sort of puts you in the spotlight. Don't you think it might be better to... well, to..."

"You mean drop out of the election?"

"After all," Nancy said quickly, "only the election committee knows that you've filed. So you could drop out without anybody being the wiser."

Stacy shook her head. "But I don't *want* to drop out," she said. "I really want to be a member of the executive council."

Nancy stood up. "Well, of course it's your decision. I'll stand by you, whatever you decide."

"I still plan to run," Stacy said, squaring her shoulders resolutely. "I don't care what people are saying. I think I would make a good officer."

Nancy flashed her a smile as she turned to go out the door. "I admire your spirit," she said. "You're the kind of person we need in Alpha Pi. Well, see ya Saturday, then, if not before."

Stacy smiled, but she knew more people than Nancy had to believe her if she was to win that election. Maybe she should have been a little more social with the sisters from the beginning. But she hadn't, and after the damage Brenda had done, it might be too late.

"Hey, Stace," Roni said. "Sam's brought a pepperoni pizza, and Terry's made some popcorn. We're pigging out—come on. It's the best ole Hawthorne Springs has to offer."

Stacy went into the living room. Pizza was out, but the popcorn sounded good, and maybe a diet cola. Terry had pulled the cushions off the blue chair, and everybody was sitting on the floor, listening to the stereo and talking.

"So what did Nancy want?" Sam asked curiously, handing Roni a piece of pizza.

Stacy sipped her soda and leaned back against the sofa. "She wanted to let me know about Brenda, Hawthorne's famous gossip columnist."

"Don't tell me," Roni said, laughing, "let me guess. Brenda went out with Alex, and they ran out of gas behind the cemetery."

"Don't I wish," Stacy said, taking the popcorn Terry handed her. She sighed.

"God, what a mess," Sam breathed. "What are we going to do?"

"I vote that we tie Brenda down and muzzle her," Roni said grimly. "She's all mouth."

"Soap," said Terry. "That's what we need. We could wash her mouth out with soap."

"Or maybe we tell everybody about Brenda's secret lover," Roni suggested with a grin. "You know, the guy she sneaks out to meet every night at midnight."

Terry stared at her openmouthed. "What guy? How do you know she sneaks out?"

"There isn't any guy, dummy," Roni said scornfully. "But we have to discredit her. You know, fight fire with fire."

"There's *got* to be a way to handle this," Sam said, pressing her fingers to her temples. "Come on, everybody, *think*!"

Stacy looked around, a lump growing in her throat. She knew these guys were her friends, and that they were trying to help, but she didn't find it very comforting. At the moment, it seemed every person at Hawthorne College distrusted her or felt sorry for her. They *felt sorry* for Stacy Swanson—the girl who had everything! If anyone had told her the day she'd decided to come to Hawthorne that this would happen, she just might have gone to Vassar.

"Uh, excuse me, please," Stacy said, hastily setting down her plate and her drink. She hobbled into her room, shut the door, and lay down on her bed.

"I don't get it," she heard Terry say through the door. "We were just trying to help."

"I think that's the problem," said Sam. "I don't think Stacy's had tons of experience needing other people—or letting them help."

Hearing that, Stacy laid her head down on her pillow and started crying. Lately it was becoming her favorite pastime.

Chapter 11

On Friday morning, Stacy took off the Ace bandage, left her crutches against her bed, and went for a walk, being careful of her sprained ankle. When she got back, she stepped on the scale. Still 113 pounds—even with all the food she'd been eating! It must have been the exercise she got from maneuvering the crutches, she decided happily. To celebrate, she put on her blue cashmere sweater, a slim gray wool skirt, and a pair of gray suede boots. She took extra care with her makeup, too, now that the black had nearly faded from her eye. She'd decided that the only way to handle this silly rumor was to look so confident that nobody would believe Alex and Brenda.

When she looked at her watch, she realized that she was going to be late to English. She'd told Pete that she'd meet him at breakfast, but it was too late

—and anyway, now that she was off her crutches, she wouldn't need him.

Stacy started walking to class, thinking how wonderful it was not to have to swing along on those ugly, awkward crutches. But halfway across the bridge someone behind her called her name. Stacy cringed when she turned and saw Brenda's round face and curious eyes.

"Oh, Stacy," she said in her Texas drawl, "it's so *good* to see you off those horrible crutches." She gave Stacy an inquisitive glance, obviously checking her out. "I do hope you're better. On Saturday you looked positively *awful*." She heaved a pitying sigh. "What an ordeal."

"Yes, spraining your ankle can be quite an ordeal," Stacy said with a slow, deliberate emphasis. "I'm glad it doesn't happen every day." She started to walk.

Brenda sighed again, falling into step with her. "I can understand why you don't want to talk about it, Stacy," she said with heavy sympathy. "I probably wouldn't either. But don't you think," she went on, "that it'd be better to get the whole thing out into the open? I mean, everybody thinks that Alex ought to be punished somehow for what he's done. He shouldn't be allowed to get away with it."

Stacy whirled toward her, anger fueling her words. "Listen, Brenda," she said, "Alex didn't *do* anything."

"Okay, okay, have it your way," Brenda agreed. "But I still think he shouldn't get away with . . ."

Stacy wasn't about to listen to any more. "I appreciate your concern, Brenda, but it's really none of your business. I have to get to class now," she said as she hurried off in the opposite direction.

When she got to Englih, the first person she saw was Roger, standing in the hall smoking a cigarette. Stacy sighed when she saw him. He *was* good-looking in that black turtleneck. It was a shame he didn't have a personality to match.

"Hey, hi!" he said, straightening up when he saw Stacy. He eyed her appreciatively. "You're looking terrific this morning, Stacy." He moved closer to her. "I mean, I like you in jeans, too, but you look great in a skirt."

Stacy stepped back, embarrassed and a little surprised by his attention. Roger was usually more reserved, or at least polite in an unusual way.

"Uh, hi," she said.

He reached over and put an arm across her shoulders. "Say, I've been thinking. I hear you're a terrific dancer, among other things." He grinned. "How'd you like to go out tonight?"

A terrific dancer? Where had he heard that? And what did he mean by "among other things"? Stacy ducked out from under his arm.

"Sorry," she said, turning to go into class. "My father's in Atlanta on business, and I'm expecting him." It wasn't much of a lie, she told herself. She *was* expecting him, although not until the next day.

Roger shoved his hand back in his pocket and gave her a lazy grin. "That's too bad," he said. "Sure you can't make it?"

"I'm sure," she said.

"Well, then, I'll take a raincheck," he said, eyeing her up and down once more and then following her into the classroom.

As she walked, she could feel Roger's gaze on her, and she blushed as a horrible thought struck her. It was stupid to think the rumors about her wouldn't go beyond Alpha Pi Alpha. She was getting to be well known on campus, but not the way she had planned.

Stacy barely heard ten words of the lecture. Afterward, she waited for a few minutes, seeing that Roger had gone before putting on her jacket. She wanted to make sure that her expression was composed. But just as she stepped out the door, she saw Pete waiting for her, his shoulder propped against the wall—so much for her composure.

"I missed you this morning, Stace," he said, "so I thought I'd better check and see if you're okay." He looked at her. "Hey, no crutches! Congratulations!"

Stacy took a deep breath. "Yeah," she said as casually as she could. "I even went for a little warm-up walk this morning. Maybe tomorrow I'll jog."

"Good for you!" He started to reach for the stack of book she held in her arms. "Listen, this calls for a celebration. How about going to the football game with me tomorrow? Maybe afterward we could go out for supper or something."

Stacy held her books tightly against her chest, and after a brief hesitation he dropped his hands, looking at her quizzically. There's wasn't any easy way to do this, she supposed. But she had to just *tell* him and get it over with. It would be less painful that way—

for both of them. Of course, it wasn't that *she* was going to be upset, but Terry was right—he was a nice guy, and it would be a shame if he got hurt.

"Listen, Pete," she said, carefully avoiding his eyes, "I'm going to be really busy in the next few weeks. My father's going to be visiting for a few days; he'll be here tomorrow. Also, we're having elections in my sorority, and I'm going to be pretty involved with the campaign." She stopped and swallowed, her mouth dry. "After that, I'll be spending the Thanksgiving holiday with my father in Boston —or maybe New York."

"So?" he asked quietly. "How's that going to change anything? I know you want to see your father, so the game's out. But we can still eat breakfast together, can't we?" He grinned. "Come on, I'll walk you to class."

Stacy hung back, trying to ignore the way her heart was pounding. "I doubt if I'll have time for breakfast—or if I do, I probably ought to eat with some of the pledges. You know, do some campaigning." She shifted uncomfortably. "I'm going to be busy the rest of the day, too. I mean, I'm still behind with my midterm work, and . . ."

There was a silence. She stole a look at him: his usual easy grin had faded, and his jaw was clenched. He turned, confronting her, his eyes intense.

"I guess there's a message somewhere in all of that for me," he said.

Mutely, Stacy nodded. Funny. There was a time when she would have enjoyed being mean to him. But now she felt an unexpected wrenching deep inside her as she read the hurt in his eyes, and she looked away uneasily.

He turned her face so she had to look at him. "Somehow I don't believe your busy schedule is all there is to it," he said, looking into her eyes. "But I guess I have to take your word for it. See you later." Then he dropped his hand and walked away. Stacy stared after him, still feeling the warmth of his hand against her cheek.

It was hard for Stacy to put the encounter with Pete out of her mind, even though she tried. She thought of him several times that day, remembering the hurt in his eyes and wishing she could do it all over again. But there was more than guilt, she was beginning to realize. There was a deep, painful ache that wouldn't go away, no matter how many times she told herself that their friendship—or whatever it was —was over. Well, the best thing she could do was to get on with the election. She simply had to win it to be in a position to stop Brenda's gossiping once and for all.

That night she couldn't get to sleep because she kept rehearsing her speech, worrying about what kind of impression she'd make. What if they hated her?

Stacy started looking for her father early the next morning; but as usual he was late—late enough to make her worry that she might have to leave for the meeting without him. But when she saw him, she was so happy that she forgave him immediately.

"Oh, Jason, it's so good to see you," she said, trying to restrain herself from acting like a child. She wanted to throw her arms around him and cover him with kisses, but that kind of affection usually put him off. She offered a cheek for him to kiss.

"Sorry I'm late, Stacy," he said, looking harried. "I took the wrong turnoff and . . ." He paused. "Hey, look at you!" He hugged her briefly, then held her at arms' length. "Hey," he said, "I like that outfit."

She was wearing a thigh-length lipstick-red sweater over a matching red skirt, with sheer black stockings, black leather boots, and a black silk scarf draped around her neck. She wanted to look absolutely perfect for the meet-the-candidates session—and, of course, she wanted to impress her father. Not an easy task.

She smiled at him. "Well, you don't look so bad yourself, Jason," she said teasingly, stepping out of his embrace.

She didn't see her father all that often—once every three or four months—but every time she did, he looked trim and handsome. Today, he was wearing a white turtleneck and a salt-and-pepper jacket. He was a little grayer than she remembered and more tired-looking. But that was probably because of last week's election. She was proud of him, and she couldn't wait to introduce him to her suitemates—and especially to the Alpha Pi's. She knew she needed help to win this election.

Jason and Stacy drove to the Alpha Pi house in the white European coupé he'd rented for the day, and Stacy was glad to see a group of Alpha Pi's standing on the veranda when she and Jason drove up. They couldn't help being impressed by the car, and immediately they began to whisper. But then Stacy thought that these girls might be the ones who'd believed Brenda—they were probably discussing her reputation as a date, not as a politician's daughter. Oh, well. She couldn't afford to worry about that right now. She had to look confident, strong, in control—whether she really felt that way or not.

As soon as the meeting began, Nancy introduced the candidates and announced that Stacy would make her presentation first.

Stacy stood up and went to the podium. Her knees were shaking, and there was a knot in her stomach. She'd met senators, governors, movie stars, and international business people, but she'd never been as nervous as she was right now. She put her notes down in front of her and began to speak as conversationally as she could.

"My name is Stacy Swanson," she said. "I come from Boston, and I went to school at Elizabeth Deere." She looked up, wondering if that would get a response. Elizabeth Deere was a *very* elite private school. Several girls nodded, and a few smiled knowingly.

"When I was in prep school," she went on, "I was on the debate team and I was secretary of the junior class. I spent a term abroad, in Switzerland"—she thought she'd just throw that in—"and I traveled all over Europe. I enjoy art and music"—she wanted them to know that she was cultured—"and my mother owns an art gallery in Beacon Hill. I've seen politics from the inside, and met a lot of interesting people, because my father is a Massachusetts state senator."

She looked up and smiled. This was her trump card. "Actually, he's here today. Jason, will you please stand up?" She gave a wave of her hand. "This is my father, everyone, Senator Jason Swanson, who has just been elected to his *fourth* term in the Massachusetts legislature."

Her father shot her a strange glance, but he stood up and bowed slightly, then waved, the way he always did to his constituents. He sat down again, and a buzz went around the room. Good, Stacy thought to herself, they're impressed!

"As you can see," she said, "my father is a successful campaigner, and he also does a good job representing his constituency in the legislature. I think I've learned a lot from him. If you elect me, I'll do my best to see that your interests are represented on the executive council." There was a wave of applause, and she sat down, sneaking a look around. Everyone seemed interested, and several of the girls were craning for a better look at her father.

Rachel, the next candidate, spoke softly and without a great deal of conviction, and Stacy had the feeling she wasn't going to be very tough competition. Laura, however, was a different matter, as Stacy realized the minute she stood up. Laura spoke crisply and succinctly, from typed notecards. She didn't say much about her background. Instead, she talked mainly about what she planned to do when she was elected to the executive council—making sure that the pledges were informed, doing things with other sororities, making Alpha Pi a better sorority. She even said that she thought pledges ought to be able to vote in the annual election. *That* suggestion brought enthusiastic applause.

Stacy frowned. She wished she'd thought of something like that. But she had a whole week to think of ideas for her program. She could come up with something just as good, she was sure of it.

When it was all over, several girls came up to say hello and wish her luck. Stacy introduced them to her father, who stood off to one side, posed in his usual stylish manner.

Nancy approached her after a few minutes. "Uh, Stacy," she said with a glance at Stacy's father, "could I see you for a minute?"

Stacy followed her into a small office just off the community room, and Nancy closed the door behind them. She looked at Stacy, her dark eyes concerned.

"Listen, Stacy, I hate to talk about this right now," she said, sitting on the edge of the desk, "but I think you'd better hear about it right away."

"Hear about what?" asked Stacy. She sat down on the chair across from the desk. "What's going on?"

"Well, I went to a party last night over at the Pi Phi house. Alex was there."

"Oh?" Stacy asked. She didn't like the look on Nancy's face.

Nancy looked down at her hands. "He'd had too

much beer, and he was . . . well, he was doing a lot of bragging. You know."

Stacy stiffened. "Bragging?"

"Yes. About the night of the hayride when you guys got lost. He was saying that you had . . . well, you know." She cleared her throat. "And he was saying it in front of a lot of guys—not just Pi Phi's, but guys from other fraternities—and some girls, too. Some of our pledges were there."

Stacy looked at her, her mouth dropping open. "I don't believe it," she gasped. "How could he? How could he . . . just *lie* like that?"

"I know," Nancy said sympathetically, "it's really bad. I mean, what some guys will do to make themselves look like real men." She leaned forward. "But even if it is a lie, Stacy, some people are bound to believe it. *They* don't know what happened. Don't you think it would be better to . . . ?"

Stacy stood up, her hands clenched tightly. "To drop out of the election?" she asked. She shook her head, madder than ever. "I'm sorry, Nancy, but I'm not going to drop out. I'm staying in this thing, and I'm going to see it through. And that's final!"

Nancy nodded. "Well, I guess I have to admire you, Stacy," she said. "And I wish you luck. You're going to need all you can get."

Chapter 12

"Stacy, I'm afraid there's something I have to tell you," her father said once they were in the car. He sat back against the door and put his elbow on the steering wheel, his face turned away. "Something I should have told you before we went in there."

"Um, what?" Stacy asked dazedly, hardly hearing him. She shook her head, still thinking about what Nancy had just told her. She hadn't believed the Alex situation could get any worse, but it had. She didn't want to know what was going to be next.

"Stacy, listen to me." Jason put his hand on her shoulder. "I need to tell you something important."

Stacy looked up, trying to focus on his face. "Something important?" If only she could tell her father what she'd just heard—*that* was something important. But she couldn't—they'd never been close. And anyway, there was nothing *he* could do.

"Yes, I'm afraid so," he said. He turned and stared through the windshield. "It's about the election. I didn't win."

"What?" She looked at her father blankly, thinking that she'd heard him wrong.

"You heard me," he said wearily. "I lost the election."

"But you've always . . . How could . . . ?"

He shrugged. "A combination of things, some of them not very pretty, I'm afraid." He grinned, but she could see the pain in the line of his mouth. "You know how complicated campaigns are, with several different people—people I don't even know—involved, working for me. It's impossible to keep track of everything."

Stacy nodded mutely.

"Well, it seems that somebody on the financial side of the campaign accepted campaign contributions from some pretty undesirable characters. Racketeer types. Unfortunately, the newspapers got wind of the damned thing before I did, and . . ."

"But who took the bribe? Somebody else—right? I mean, it wasn't you."

"No, it wasn't me. I want you to believe that, Stacy. But, I was implicated because I was the candidate. I knew the week before the election that we didn't stand a chance, but I went through with it anyway."

"But I still don't understand. Do you mean to tell me that you're not—"

"Right. I'm not Senator Jason Swanson. At least,

not after January." He rested his forehead against the wheel.

She leaned forward and put her hand on his head. Funny, it was the first time she'd seen one of her parents look defeated. "It's okay," she whispered shakily, wishing she could believe what she was saying. "It's going to be okay, Jason."

After a minute he straightened up, his eyes bright with tears. "I wish I had your optimism." He sighed. "It's not going to be easy." He straightened his shoulders a little. "Of course, I've got options. There's still the law firm. Or I could move to New York and go into partnership with Morse." Morse Swanson was his brother, an attorney.

Stacy nodded, trying to make herself sound confident. "Of course, Jason. You can do anything, so I'm sure you can get another great job. Morse would be glad to have you. I know what," she said. "At Thanksgiving, let's go to New York. You can talk to Morse, and I can do some shopping, and we'll have a wonderful time." She smiled softly. It would be the first time she and her father could get away together —it would be the trip they'd missed at graduation.

"Thanksgiving?" Her father looked at her. "Listen, Stacy, I'm afraid you're going to have to be on your own for this holiday."

"On my own? But I don't . . ."

"Now that the election's over, I need to get away —far away—for a while. Some friends of mine have a condo in Colorado, and I'm gong to go there for a couple of weeks." He looked at his watch. "It's getting late. I've got to get back to the city." He put the key in the ignition, and started the car.

"Late? It's early afternoon! And what do you mean, get back to the city?" Stacy exclaimed, dismayed. "I thought we were going to the football game."

Jason turned out of the drive. "I know I should have told you earlier so you could make your plans. I hope you're not upset. I don't think I'd be very good company, anyway."

Stacy looked out the window. "I don't know," she said. "Maybe it would be a good time for us to be together. My life hasn't exactly been great lately, either. And we could kind of get to know one another better."

He laughed shortly as he turned the corner. "A little late for that, don't you think?"

The remark, delivered with such nonchalance, stung Stacy. "No, I *don't* think it's too late," she retorted. "I mean, you *are* my father, after all." She turned toward him, a new idea forming in her mind. "Colorado isn't *that* far away. How about if I fly to Denver for a few days?"

"That wouldn't be a very good idea, Stacy," he said. "The truth is that I'll be with someone else—a new, very important, very lovely friend."

"But that doesn't matter," Stacy protested. "I mean, I've been with you when your girlfriends have been along. There was that time we went to England and—"

"I know," her father said quietly. He pulled the car into the Rogers House lot. "I remember. But it's a little different this time. You see, Susan is . . ." He took a deep breath, looking a little sheepish. "Actually, Susan is only a year older than you are, Stacy. She's a sophomore at BU." He cleared his throat uncomfortably. "She's very mature for her age, and sophisticated, and . . . well, the problem is that I haven't gotten around to telling her about *you* just yet."

After Jason drove off, Stacy walked toward the lake and stood looking out at the water. The air was crisp and autumnlike, but the breeze chilled her to the bone. The sky was laced with clouds, and the lake shimmered with blue and silver. Over at the stadium, the Hawthorne band was beginning to play the pregame warm-up, and the bridge was crowded with students on their way to the game, laughing and cheering and waving pennants. But Stacy wasn't in the mood for fun. She shivered. She could have handled Brenda's silly rumor by ignoring it, and it would have died away as soon as the next sensational thing occurred. But what could she do about Alex? And on top of that, there was the scandal back in Boston. The Swanson name must be all over the headlines. And then there was Jason's other news. She couldn't spend Thanksgiving with her own father because he was going to be spending it with somebody else—a girl her own age!

In the distance, she heard a whistle and the roar of the crowd. She was late for kick-off. She thrust her hands into her pockets and started around the lake.

Before she knew where she was going, Stacy

found herself standing in front of the Fine Arts Complex. At least she could work on her pottery without being bombarded with bad news. She went to her locker and changed into her clay-stained overalls, then took her tools into the deserted studio. But her hands felt clumsy and awkward, and her third effort turned into a crooked lump of gray mud. Couldn't she do anything right? She sat there for a moment, staring at the ruined clay, trying to hold back the tears of self-pity that prickled behind her eyelids. She refused to cry again.

"Feel like taking a break?"

It was Pete, standing beside her holding out a can of diet soda. "Thanks," she said, taking it. Her heart started to jump, but she tried to stay calm. "What're you doing here?" she asked casually, not looking at him. "I thought you were going to the game."

"I was there, but I came to check the kiln. We're firing today." He paused. "I talked to your roommates just before halftime," he said quietly. "They were looking for you and your father." He gave her an inquiring look. "He had to go back to Atlanta, huh?"

"Yeah, he went back," Stacy said in a low voice. "He's on his way to Colorado—with his girlfriend." She stopped. Why was she telling this to Pete?

"Oh," Pete said. "I see." He cleared his throat. "Well, I guess he's entitled. I mean, after winning the election, he must be ready for a few days' rest."

"He didn't win."

Pete raised an eyebrow. "Really? What happened?"

"Somebody in his campaign took money from somebody crooked. Of course, it's all over the papers up there. Thank God the Hawthorne Springs *Examiner* is such a funky little paper. At least they won't carry the story."

"Well," Pete said cheerfully, "at least you'll be able to spend Thanksgiving in a great place. Will you be in Denver, Vail or Aspen?"

"I'm not going." There was a roar from the crowd at the stadium and a whistle. "Listen," Stacy said, "the second half's starting. You're late."

"I don't care about the game." Pete put his hand on her shoulder, looking at her intently. "How come you're not going?"

"Because he doesn't want me to," Stacy said miserably. "He hasn't told his girlfriend about me yet. She's . . . she's a sophomore at BU." She laughed bitterly. "A sophomore. Can you believe it?"

"Hey," Pete said, reaching for her hand. "I hate to say it, but it's his business who he sees. As hard as it is for you, he has a whole other life that you can't always be a part of."

"I know," Stacy said. "But a *sophomore*?" Pete's hand felt firm and comforting in hers. "God," she whispered, "everything's coming apart."

Pete's grip tightened. "I know you're having a rough time, what with those stupid rumors and problems with classes, but you'll make it, Stacy. You just have to be yourself, and everybody will understand the real—"

Stacy pulled back, startled. "The rumors? How did you know about that?"

He looked at her squarely. "That guy in your English class—Roger? I ran into him yesterday, and he made some smart remark to me. So I asked Terry about it, at the game. It seems that she'd just told Brenda off." He grinned. "I'll bet Brenda doesn't open her mouth again for a while. That ought to settle the rumors down. All you have to do is ignore it and—"

"But I can't ignore it," she whispered. "Not now." She knew she shouldn't be telling all this to Pete, but he was so understanding. He'd already heard the rumors, and he still liked her and believed in her. And she really needed to talk to somebody. "The trouble is that Alex—the guy I went out with—is telling everybody that the rumors are true."

Pete stared at her. "Are you sure? How do you know?"

"Nancy—the Alpha Pi president—told me." Stacy knew she was going to burst into tears—she couldn't help it. "He was drunk, and a whole bunch of frat brothers heard him."

"Ssh." Pete folded her in his arms and pulled her against him. "Don't cry. Maybe a few people will be fooled, but the smart ones will know he's just trying to impress them." He put his lips against her hair. "It'll be okay," he whispered.

For a moment, Stacy relaxed against him, letting the tears flow, feeling the comfort of his strong arms around her, the warmth of his reassurance. It seemed *right*, somehow. And when he lowered his lips to hers and kissed her, slowly and gently, that seemed right, too.

But the kiss suddenly jarred Stacy back to reality. This couldn't be! It was wrong, all wrong! She couldn't lose control this way, couldn't let Pete see how much she hurt or how vulnerable she was. She pulled away awkwardly, straightening her shoulders. "Yeah," she said, "it'll be okay." She picked up her clay tools and started back to her locker.

Pete followed her. "Stacy," he said, his voice very serious, "Why don't you let your friends help you out?"

"Because I don't *need* help," Stacy said, gritting her teeth. "And I certainly don't need anybody—including you—to feel sorry for me. Please just go away and leave me alone for once!"

"I guess maybe I should," Pete said very quietly. He turned and walked away.

Stacy stormed down the hallway, muttering to herself. "Let someone carry your books, and they think they *own* you. I mean, is this college or grade school? Really."

Chapter 13

On Sunday evening, the Alpha Pi's were having a reception. Stacy didn't want to go—she still felt pretty lousy about yesterday—but if she stayed away, people would probably gossip about where she was. Anyway, she had to start campaigning. Winning the election now seemed more important to her than ever before. She *had* to show everybody that she could win, in spite of the ugly things people were saying. So she put on a burgundy silk dress and her best pearls and practiced smiling.

At the reception, several girls told her that they liked her presentation, and they asked her questions about herself and what she thought the executive council ought to be doing. But she noticed that Laura, the other candidate, seemed to know everybody far better than Stacy did—she was collecting a big crowd around her. And she also noticed that some of the girls were looking at her constantly and whispering among themselves. Her face was red with embarrassment, and she could only hope that people thought it was the reflection from her dress.

"Hi, Stacy." Stacy turned around. It was Lisa, a pledge who lived next door to Brenda in Rogers House. "I didn't see you and your father at the game yesterday. Did he have to leave?"

"Oh, hi, Lisa," Stacy said carelessly. "Yes, he had an early flight. He couldn't stay."

Lisa shifted from one foot to the other. "It must be very interesting, having a senator for a father," she said. "And especially one who's won so many elections. Didn't you say he'd been elected to four terms?"

"Uh, yes, that's what I said," she replied. Hurriedly, she changed the subject. "What do you think about Alpha Pi getting together with the Pi Phi's to put on a benefit?" she asked. Several other girls had come up to join the conversation, and for the next few minutes Stacy was busy answering questions about what she'd do if she were on the executive council. When she looked around again, Lisa had disappeared.

On Tuesday, Stacy got her campaign flyers back from the copy center and made her first door-to-door call on a pledge who lived in Rogers, on the third floor. "Hi, Megan," she said nervously when the girl answered the door. "If you've got a few minutes, I'd like to talk about the Alpha Pi election."

Megan opened the door farther. "Sure," she said with a friendly smile. "How's the campaign going?"

"Okay, thanks," said Stacy. "Here's my flyer—let me tell you the kinds of things I think the executive council ought to be doing. I've got some ideas, especially about better communication—keeping everybody informed about what's going on." They talked for a few minutes, and then Stacy went to see the next pledge, feeling confident. If all her calls were as easy and friendly as *that* one, she'd be sure to win.

But some of the girls said they didn't have time, or they just let her talk without really listening. She knew that the girls on Brenda's floor would be the hardest, and she saved them until last. They were friendly enough, but they looked at her knowingly. She could almost read what was in their minds, and when she was done, she knew she hadn't been exaggerating things. A lot of people had heard Brenda's gossip and Alex's lies, and worse, a lot of people obviously *believed* what they'd heard. She came back to the suite even more depressed than ever and picked Bandit up, cuddling him close. She was so sick of being talked about for all the wrong reasons. Didn't people have anything better to do?

Just before English class on Wednesday, Roger approached her. This was the first time she'd seen him since Pete had told her about his "complimentary" remark. She blushed when she saw him and bent intently over her book.

"Hi there, beautiful," he said in what he obviously thought was a sexy voice. He bent down close to her ear and whispered, "Listen, how about—"

Stacy didn't let him finish. "Roger," she said, closing her book, "I know what you've heard. I know what Alex is saying. But it isn't true. You are barking up the wrong tree." She opened her book again. "So go away, huh?"

"But—but—" Roger sputtered. "I didn't mean . . . that is . . . Oh, never mind," he said, and shoved his hands in his pockets.

Stacy looked up from her book again. Roger's face was deep scarlet, and he actually looked embarrassed. "Good," she said with the sweetest smile she could muster. "I *knew* you'd understand."

Roger went to his seat and slouched down into it as far as he could. For the first time in a long while, Stacy felt good.

On Thursday, the weather suddenly turned cold and crisp, and there were sprinkles of snow in the air. The kids in the dorm were all talking about going home for Thanksgiving, and Stacy felt lonely and left out, as if everyone else in the world had gotten an invitation to some terrific party—everyone, that is, except her. But Sam, Roni, and Terry all seemed to be in competition to get her to go home with them, and if anything could have made her feel better, *that* did. Their efforts reached a climax when Sam's mother called on Thursday night with a special personal invitation to Stacy.

"We really want you to come," said Mrs. Hill. "In fact, we're counting on it."

Beside Stacy, with her ear pressed to the phone,

Sam nodded vehemently. "You tell her, Mom," she cheered into the phone.

"Thanks, Mrs. Hill," Stacy said, hoping she didn't sound ungrateful. "But I've got a lot of catching up to do, and I've decided to stay on campus." To herself she had to admit that she didn't really want to spend Thanksgiving Day in an empty dorm. But she didn't want to be with a borrowed family, either, watching all the love and warmth that families always generated on such special days. She already felt like an outsider—and that would only make it worse. So she just had to say no, thank you.

On the day of the Alpha Pi election, Stacy walked to the sorority house at four, after she'd finished making up her last music quiz. She was so deep in thought that she didn't realize she was walking behind three Alpha Pi pledges until she'd almost caught up with them. She was just about to say hello when she overheard what they were saying.

"I honestly didn't believe it when I read the clipping my mother sent from the Boston *Herald*." It was Lisa, the girl who'd asked Stacy earlier about her father. "I mean, Stacy actually *said* he been elected. She *lied* about it. The papers are full of the scandal. Everybody in Boston is saying that Jason Swanson actually took money from gangsters."

"I don't understand," said the second girl, shaking her head. "How come she went out of her way to introduce him to us if she knew—"

She was interrupted by a third girl, one of Brenda's suitemates. "Well, you've got to admit," she said snidely, "that Stacy's been involved with some pretty weird things lately. That ugly thing with Alex, now this stuff about her father—some of the girls are even saying that she's anorexic."

"I'm not surprised," the first girl said. "She's so thin she's hardly even pretty. She's got terrific clothes —God, I *envy* her clothes—but they don't even look good on her."

"Well, I don't really *care* what she does," said the third girl, "I'm going to vote for Laura. All I can think of is that time Stacy bragged about owning a new Mercedes. I mean, a Mercedes is a terrific car, but if you go around advertising that you've got one, you must be desperate, or trying too hard—or else just an incredible snob. Don't you think?"

Stacy listened with growing horror as the girls talked. All of the rumors were mounting up, accumulating—now nobody liked her. And the harder she tried to make things better, the worse they got. It was like being trapped in an awful nightmare—only it wasn't a nightmare, it was her life.

She voted quickly and came back to the suite, almost in a daze. What she had heard was enough to let her know that she *couldn't* win the election, no matter what. It was dark outside, and a chill drizzle had begun, but she put on her running clothes and went for a long run—around the lake and out onto Grove Street, down to the Civil War monument, and then back to the gym and around the lake again. She ran hard, hearing the pounding of the blood in her ears, feeling out of breath, exhausted, but unable to stop. By the time she got back to the suite, she was thoroughly soaked and chilled.

"God, Stacy, what have you been doing?" Terry exclaimed when Stacy stumbled into the suite. She dropped her chemistry book and stood up from the sofa. "Where've you been? Nancy's been calling all evening."

Stacy fell onto the sofa, gasping for breath. "I don't want to talk to her," she said, covering her face with her hands. "I don't want to talk to anybody."

"Well, you don't need to worry about that for right now," Terry said firmly. "You're getting into the shower this minute, before you come down with pneumonia. For goodness' sake, Stacy, you can't keep punishing your body this way." She pulled Stacy up and shoved her toward the bathroom. "Get in there."

Stacy stood in the shower for a long time, letting the hot water warm her chilled bones. She heard the telephone ring and hoped it wasn't Nancy again. She *knew* why Nancy was calling—to tell her that Laura had been elected to the executive council in a landslide. She'd be lucky if she'd gotten even a handful of votes.

Stacy went back into the living room wrapped in her pink robe, and Terry handed her a cup of hot chocolate. "Sit down," she commanded, "and drink that. And I don't want to hear a word about calories. Not a single word."

Stacy sat down and took a sip. Anorexic, that's what the girl had said. But she only wanted to keep her weight down. "So thin she isn't even pretty?" She shivered. Was the girl really talking about *her*? She wasn't *thin*, she was just *slender*.

There was a knock at the door. Stacy didn't want to see anybody, but Terry got up and opened the door. It was Nancy, wearing a yellow slicker that glistened with rain.

"You didn't have to come over here in the rain, Nancy," Stacy said. "You could have just left a message. I'd have understood."

Nancy took off her slicker and stood the umbrella up in a corner. "I wanted to let you know what the election committee decided tonight," she said, taking the cup of hot chocolate Terry handed her.

"Laura won, didn't she?"

"Yes," Nancy said. She sat down on the sofa. "She did win. But it was close, Stacy. You got a lot of votes."

It was close? Stacy thought Nancy must be kidding. Well, maybe not *everybody* thought she was a promiscuous snob whose father took money from gangsters. There was hope.

Nancy looked at Stacy. "But the girls on the committee have talked about the situation, and we've decided to change the way the pledge class is organized."

"Change it?"

"We want to have a pledge advisory board, Stacy. It would be experimental, until we see how it works. We want all three of you to be on it—you and Rachel and Laura. Laura will still be the representative to the executive council, but this way all three of you can be involved."

Stacy shook her head, wrapping her hands around her mug. "It's a big change," she said, "and you're only doing it because you feel sorry for me. I can't accept that."

"It's not that big a change," Nancy replied. "And it *isn't* just for you. We talked about it last year, but we weren't exactly sure how it would work. This year, because we have three strong candidates and the election was so close, we'd like to give it a try."

Stacy shook her head. She couldn't help but be touched by Nancy's concern, but it was too much like a consolation prize.

Nancy put down her cup. "You don't have to tell me tonight, Stacy," she said. "In fact, we don't plan to put this new idea into effect until after Thanksgiving." She leaned over and gave Stacy a hug. "Listen, I know how you're feeling, Stacy," she said. "I'd feel the same way. But did a terrific job, under really difficult circumstances, and I hope you'll be on the board. Will you at least think about it?"

Reluctantly, Stacy nodded. She'd think about it for Nancy's sake. But she was pretty sure she knew what her answer would be. Nancy put her slicker on and turned to Stacy. "Think hard," she said, and left.

Later that night, while Stacy was sleeping peacefully, Sam came into the suite at about two o'clock in the morning, with Aaron. Bandit, awakened by Stacy's stirring, scampered off the bed and ran out the door into the living room, where Sam and Aaron were talking in low voices. After a few minutes,

Stacy heard the door shut, and then it was silent. Sam must have walked downstairs to say good night to Aaron. Stacy rolled over and tried to go back to sleep.

But suddenly she heard a loud scream in the hallway, followed by a loud banging. She grabbed her robe and ran to the door.

"What is it?" Terry gasped, right behind Stacy. "Is it a fire? What's going on?"

"I don't hear the alarm," Stacy said. Cautiously, she opened the door. Karen Smith from suite 2D was out in the hallway with Patty, her suitemate.

"He's all bloody," Karen was saying. "And look, his paw is hurt."

"I can't believe this little kitten killed that big mouse!" exclaimed Patty. "Whose kitten *is* this, anyway? Where did he come from?"

Stacy ran into the hall. "Kitten!" she cried. "Bandit? Bandit, are you all right?" She looked down at Bandit, who was calmly licking a bloody paw. In front of him lay an ugly brown mouse as big as he was, with a long, hairless tail and spiky teeth—very bloody and *very* dead.

"Yuk, gross," said Terry, coming to stand beside Stacy. "What an *ugly* mouse. He's huge! He looks abnormal. How did Bandit do it?"

"I think that's the same mouse that's been eating my granola," Patty said. "No wonder he's so big. I set a trap, but he stole the bait." She looked at Stacy. "Is the cat yours, Stacy?"

"Well, uh, actually..." Stacy began.

"Actually, he's *ours*," Terry broke in. "He's sort of

a community cat, you might say." She picked Bandit up and began to examine his bloody paw.

Stacy stared at Terry in surprise. After all the times she's wanted to get rid of Bandit!

"What happened?" Sam asked, walking up the hall. She looked at Bandit in Terry's arms. "Oh, no," she said guiltily. "I must have left the door open and he got out."

"Well, it's a good thing he did," Patty remarked. "He killed the mouse that's been eating my granola."

"I think we ought to award him the Purple Cross," Karen said, "and hire him to clean up this dorm." She shook her head. "Rogers is overrun with mice."

"What's going on out here?" a grumpy voice said. "Don't you girls know that it's two in the morning? What's all this racket?"

"It's Pam!" Stacy breathed into Terry's ear. "Quick, hide Bandit!"

Frantically, Terry tried to stuff Bandit under her robe, but it was too late. Pam was standing at her elbow, looking from Bandit down to the mouse, lying dead on the floor.

"You don't mean to tell me that this tiny kitten killed *that* mouse," she said in an awed voice.

"World-champion mouser," Karen said. "I vote for keeping him on duty."

"Whose cat *is* this?" Pam demanded, looking at everyone.

"He's ours," Terry spoke up quickly with a glance at Stacy. "He belongs to suite two C—to all of us."

Stacy swallowed. She was grateful to Terry for sharing the responsibility, but she couldn't let everyone get into trouble on her account. "No, it's my fault," she confessed. "I'm the one. Don't blame the others."

Pam held out a finger, and Bandit licked it. "I'm not blaming anyone," she said. "But you know the rules. No pets in the dorm."

"Yes, I know," Stacy said sadly. Was she really going to lose Bandit, on top of everything else?

"Listen, Pam," said Sam, "we'll make him an *invisible* cat. He'll stay in the suite and nobody will know. . . ."

"Couldn't you make an exception?" Terry pleaded. She pointed to the mouse. "This kitten should get a medal, not an eviction notice."

"That's right," Patty chimed in. "Rogers *needs* a good mouser."

"I'm sorry, girls," Pam replied, pulling her robe around her. "I don't have any choice. He's got to be out of here by the time you come back from the holiday. That's all there is to it."

With a sinking heart, Stacy carried Bandit back into the suite and took him into the bathroom to wash the blood off his hurt paw. So much had happened in the last few days that losing Bandit seemed like the last straw. She sat down on the edge of the bathtub with Bandit on her lap and cuddled him against her.

Chapter 14

The campus was half-empty by Tuesday morning, and the teachers were complaining about students taking an extra day of vacation. At noon, just before the bookstore closed for the holiday, Stacy stopped to get some paper. She was standing in line at the checkout when she heard a familiar voice behind her.

"Hi, Stacy," Pete said softly. He looked steadily at her, and the pain in his eyes was so obvious that Stacy had to look away.

"Uh, hi," she said, and looked ahead. There were two people in front of her: she was trapped. Why did this have to happen? she asked herself. She was just managing to put Pete Young out of her mind, and now here he was. She couldn't help remembering the last time they had been together and the way his arms had felt around her.

"You . . . you're getting ready to go away for the

holiday?" he asked. He shifted from one foot to the other. "I suppose you're going home with one of your roommates." He was making small talk—not much else.

"No," she said, "I'm staying here." She tried a small smile. "They offered, but I didn't feel like borrowing a family after mine folded on me." She stopped. What *was* there about Pete that made her say such unexpected, revealing things? She dropped the paper onto a shelf beside her. "I guess I don't need this," she muttered. "I can always borrow some of Sam's paper." And with that she bolted out the door, not wanting to prolong the agony.

Stacy said good-bye to Roni, the last one to leave, on Wednesday morning. Everybody else was gone, and Rogers House was silent for the first time since Stacy had arrived at Hawthorne. She and Bandit were the only ones in the whole dorm, and there was an almost eerie silence about the place. Bandit curled up on a chair and napped while Stacy pulled on a pair of faded jeans and Roni's old red long-john shirt. There was no need to dress up, since there was nobody around. She went into the deserted living room, feeling a sudden aching loneliness. Everybody else in the whole world was having a wonderful time this Thanksgiving—everybody except her. It had been a miserable semester. Everything was a mess— she'd completely lost control of her life. And now, to cap it all off, here she was, all by herself, for the entire Thanksgiving holiday.

She looked across the room. Taped to the refrigerator door was a note. FOR FURTHER IN-STRUCTIONS, it said in big red letters, LOOK UNDER RONI'S BED.

Stacy went into Roni's room and looked under the bed. There was a big cardboard box: on it was written, in Roni's favorite dark plum lipstick, STACY'S SURVIVAL KIT. Stacy took the box into the living room and sat down on the sofa and opened it. Inside were half a dozen newspaper-wrapped packages and another note.

Dear Stacy,
This is a *CARE* package for you, and you only. No cats allowed. We want you to survive without us—as impossible as that sounds. Unwrap one of these packages every morning until we get back on Sunday. But if you can't wait, open everything now, and don't feel guilty. Just enjoy. We'll be thinking of you.

Love,
Roni, Sam, and Terry

Stacy stared at the note, suddenly stung. This was too much. Roni, Sam and Terry felt *sorry* for her. They *pitied* her. She could just imagine how they'd giggled and laughed, getting all their silly little gifts together to lift "poor Stacy" out of the dumps. She crumpled up the note and threw it, as hard as she could, across the room. Then tears suddenly overwhelmed her, dissolving her anger. Of course they felt sorry for her. The whole situation was pretty pathetic. She was alone because her parents didn't want her, and they didn't care how she felt about it. Her suitemates had only tried to brighten that loneliness. She sank back on the sofa and let the tears come.

After a few minutes, Stacy picked up the first package. Something tinkled in it. When she opened it, she found a little bell. The card said, "To summon your fairy godmother, who will answer your every wish—or bring your Prince Charming—whichever." It was signed Roni.

Sadly, Stacy tinkled the bell. It would have to have some pretty powerful magic to solve *her* problems. She looked at the other packages, then began to pull off the paper. Of course she couldn't wait—they'd known that, and she smiled a little. The second package contained a little plastic pig, from Terry, with a sign around his neck that read, "Pig Out!" and a dollar-off coupon from PizzaRoo. The third contained a white stuffed kitty, about the size of Bandit, from Sam, and a tiny plastic mouse. The last three packages were all edible, with the note "The Next Best Thing to Being There": a package of turkey bologna, a box of Stove-Top Stuffing Mix, and a can of cranberry sauce with a clove-studded orange on top.

Stacy looked at the gift-laden coffee table. She didn't *deserve* such marvelous friends! Her parents might not love her, her sorority sisters might think she was a snob, but she had wonderful suitemates, in spite of the way she'd acted all semester. She'd snubbed Sam, snapped at Terry, and made fun of Roni—but she was only human after all, and this was the first time she'd lived with three girls her own age. She was adjusting. And it was definitely worth the trouble.

There was a knock on the door, and Stacy got up. She must look a mess, with her sloppy clothes and her uncombed hair. Oh, well, it was probably only Roni, coming back for something she'd forgotten.

But when she opened the door, it *wasn't* Roni. It was Pete, lounging against the door jamb with his hands in his pockets. He had on a blue jean jacket and a red muffler, and there was a package under his arm. She stared at him for a moment, confused.

"You didn't take this with you yesterday," he said, holding out the package of paper she'd left at the bookstore. "I figured maybe you'd run out of something to write on."

"Thanks," Stacy said, "but I really don't need—"

"I know," Pete interrupted, looking straight at her. "You don't need the paper, you don't need your roommates, you don't need friends, you don't need *me*. All you need is Stacy Swanson." His voice had a jagged edge, and he wasn't smiling. "Can I come in? It's cold out here in the hall. I think they've turned the heat off." He elbowed his way past her.

"Hey, wait," Stacy sputtered, following him into the room. "What gives you the right to barge in here and talk to me like . . ."

He was staring at her. "You've been crying," he said, more gently.

"I have not," Stacy said. She put her hand up to her cheek.

"Are you crying because you're lonely, or because you're feeling sorry for yourself?"

Stacy clenched her fists. What a horrible thing for him to say! "You'd feel sorry for yourself, too, if your parents as much as told you they didn't want you around, and you were eating turkey bologna for your Thanksgiving dinner."

"Yeah," Pete said, "I probably would." He grinned a little. "But I guess I'd try to do something about it."

"*Do* something about it!" Stacy glared at him. She folded her arms across her chest and tapped her foot. "Okay, if you're so smart, Pete Young, just what would you *do*?"

"Well, for starters," he said calmly, "I wouldn't hang around an empty dormitory by myself all weekend, feeling depressed. If a friend asked me over for dinner, I'd go." He looked at her. "I'm asking."

Stacy frowned. "Asking what?"

"Asking you over for Thanksgiving dinner. To my house. With my family."

"I *told* you," Stacy said emphatically, "I've had plenty of offers. But I don't want to borrow a family. I don't want—"

"Yeah, I know. You don't want to feel better. You'd rather hang around here and feel sorry for yourself." He paused, studying her, his head tilted to one side. "You know, I'll just bet that more than anything, you're afraid."

"Afraid?" Stacy exclaimed scornfully. "Afraid of what? What have I got to be afraid of?"

"Afraid you'll relax and let yourself go, afraid

you'll lose control for a change." He paused, watching her. "Afraid you'll show somebody who Stacy Swanson really is, behind her bank account and her fancy prep school diploma and her designer clothes."

Stacy stared at him openmouthed, her scornful defensiveness threatening to dissolve beneath his steady gaze. God, that was cruel. How dare he—how *could* he be so cruel? But it was close, and it *hurt*! She put her hands over her ears, and Pete pulled them away.

"You know what your problem is, Stacy?" he continued relentlessly. The lines around his mouth were taut, and his eyes were narrowed. "Your problem is that you've got a whole drawerful of convenient labels that you stick on people when you first meet them. Blue for acceptable people, red for unacceptable." He laughed a little harshly. "Yeah, I know. I'm wearing one of your red labels. I'm work-study, I'm a townie, and I don't belong to a fraternity. And you've got a blue label—you're an Alpha Pi who drives her own Mercedes, buys her clothes in Paris, and never misses the opening of the opera season back in Boston." He leaned closer, still holding her hands. "Am I right, Stacy? Or is there more to you —and me—than that? I think so. I certainly hope so, anyway."

Stacy stared at him. Nobody had ever dared talk to her this way, never in her whole life. She ought to be angry at him for being so presumptuous, she ought to be insulted—yes, she ought to throw him out! But she knew in her heart that he was right. And she didn't exactly want him to leave—she needed him right now. That knowledge was almost as disturbing as the things he was saying.

She jerked her hands away from his and took a step backward. "I'm not going to listen to this," she snapped. "You don't have any right to say those things."

"Are they true?"

Stacy looked down. "That doesn't matter."

Pete lifted her chin so that she had to look at him. "I think it *does* matter," he said. "Of course, you can go on lying about how you feel. You can lie to your roommates, you can lie to me." He shook his head. "But if you lie to yourself, you're *really* in trouble. You might be digging a hole so deep you'll never be able to get out."

Stacy swallowed. Looking back, over the semester and over her life, she had to admit that he could be right. It had always been hard for her to get close to people. But was it because she didn't want them to find out what was inside her? Or was it that *she* didn't want to find out what was in there? It hurt to admit it, even to herself. There wasn't anything she could do to change things, even if he was right. She was what she was. People didn't just stop being who they were and become someone different just because somebody waved a magic wand or tinkled a little bell. That was okay for Cinderella maybe, but it didn't happen that way in real life.

"So just what do you think I should do?" she asked in a taunting voice. "What's your prescription, Dr. Young?"

Pete shrugged. "Just relax a little," he said. "Let

go of that iron-fisted control you keep over yourself all the time. Let people see more of the Stacy who's really sweet and tender but who's held in check by the Stacy who needs to show everybody how absolutely *perfect* she is." His mouth softened, and he touched her cheek tenderly. "You haven't been perfect this morning," he said, "and I, for one, like you just the same."

Stacy took a deep breath. "Is there anything else?" she asked sarcastically. "Are you sure you haven't forgotten anything?"

Pete dropped his hand. "Well, I guess I wish you'd reserve judgment about me long enough to figure out whether I'm worth liking on my own terms. That's all."

Stacy laughed shakily, trying to regain her composure. "You're not asking much, are you?" Letting go, relaxing, giving people a glimpse of the not-so-perfect Stacy—that was probably the biggest challenge she had been handed in her whole life. And here it was, delivered in a slow southern drawl by a presumptuous, insulting boy she'd only met a few weeks ago.

For a moment Pete stood there, looking at her. "Yeah, I know," he said. "It's a pretty tall order. But nobody's going to flunk you if you try and it doesn't work." He grinned and stepped backward. "So how about dinner tomorrow? My mom guarantees the biggest turkey in Hawthorne Springs, with honey yams and a couple of pumpkin pies, southern style. And the nicest, craziest family you'll ever meet. Also southern style." He laughed, then studied her face intently. "You up to it, Stacy?"

Stacy hesitated. What was she risking? Everything else in her life had already fallen apart. Besides, deep down, she loved a challenge. And how could she say no to Pete Young? He was so convincing that she'd almost eaten grits and gravy once.

"I don't know whether I'm up to it or not," she said honestly. "But I don't have much to lose, do I? Believe it or not, I like pumpkin pie even more than I like yogurt."

"See? I knew you were keeping secrets from me," Pete said in a mock serious tone.

Stacy laughed. "I've got to study all day today, though, if I'm actually going to be on holiday tomorrow. So is it okay if I'm rude one last time?"

"Just as long as it's the last time. Bandit here will be our witness. I'll see you tomorrow, Stace. Hit those books!"

"I'll hit *you* if you don't leave now," Stacy said as she closed the door on Pete. "Bye."

Chapter 15

Pete came to get Stacy at eleven on Thanksgiving morning in a battered Ford pickup truck painted gray. Snow was falling lightly, and for the first time it really seemed like a holiday to her.

She stood and stared at the truck apprehensively. "I've never ridden in a pickup before."

"Well, then, you haven't *lived*," Pete said, opening the door for her. "It's an experience you'll never forget."

Stacy looked around as she clambered onto the high seat. "I'm sure."

Pete got in and patted the dash affectionately. "Just be nice to this old truck, and we'll get there." He turned the key and then switched on the windshield wipers. "I told you it snows in Georgia, didn't I? How do you like it?"

"I *love* it," she said. "It's beautiful." Big flakes

153

were drifting down from the sky and clinging like confectionery sugar to the tips of the pine boughs.

"I love it, too," said Pete, turning the corner, "as long as it doesn't get any deeper. You might do something silly like sprain your ankle again. Then I'd have to help you over the snow drift with your crutches. So be careful. I don't aim to carry your twenty-five pound textbooks *all* year." He grinned at her.

Stacy smiled and leaned against the seat. "If I were you, I wouldn't worry about me walking in this snow—I'd worry about you driving this ancient truck in it." They both laughed. Stacy appreciated his efforts to make her relax. She'd thought and thought about the things he'd said yesterday, and although she hated to admit it, she was beginning to think he could be right. She had always needed to have things her own way—maybe as a way of making up for the family she had missed. But she was beginning to see that her insistence on things and people being perfect meant she could never be happy. But could she change? She wasn't sure. There was a big difference between knowing that you ought to do something and being able to do it.

Pete's house was a rambling Victorian that sat on a little hill. He parked the truck out front, and they went up the front walk, picking their way over a litter of bicycles and skateboards. There was a huge wreath on the door.

"My mom's the holiday type," Pete told her. He opened the door, and they were met by the rich odor of turkey. "And if there's no holiday to celebrate, there's always birthdays."

With a family the size of the Young family, she could see what he meant by "there's always birthdays." He had two brothers and four sisters, all younger. There was an eighteen-month-old girl with red hair who had oatmeal on her face. There were the seven-year-old twins—Stacy couldn't tell them apart until one fell down the stairs and blacked his eye—a tomboyish girl about ten wearing Indian paint and carrying a slingshot in her back pocket, and a seventeen-year-old girl named Alice who immediately asked Stacy how she could get into Alpha Pi when she went to Hawthorne. Pete's fifteen-year-old sister, Margaret, had brought her boyfriend home for the holidays. The Youngs even had two dogs and a calico cat.

In addition to Pete's brothers and sisters, there were what seemed like dozens of assorted aunts and uncles, cousins, and a couple of grandparents. There was a lot of back-slapping and hugging as the relatives began to gather in the living room, where Mr. Young had built a roaring fire in the brick fireplace. Everybody was wearing jeans and sweaters and Stacy felt uncomfortably overdressed in her white ruffled blouse and pearls. Pete had disappeared into the backyard, so she followed Alice into the living room and sat beside her on the sofa, wishing she could go home and change. Or maybe, she thought, squirming uncomfortably as the noise level climbed, just go home and *stay*.

"You're pretty." One of the twins clambered onto her lap with a grape jelly sandwich and gave her a sticky hug. "Are you Pete's girlfriend?"

Stacy blushed. "I don't think so," she said as the twin jumped off and ran away.

Alice laughed. "I see you've been initiated into the Young clan," she said, pointing at Stacy's blouse.

Stacy stared down at herself and saw, to her dismay, that the twin had left a big purple smear on the front. What would everyone think?

But nobody seemed to think that anything was out of the way—in fact, quite the opposite. "I see that one of the twins has left his stamp of approval on you," Pete's father said with a warm twinkle, turning away from the fireplace. "They only do it to people with nice laps who like to hug."

"Yeah, watch it," said one of the cousins. "If they like you too much, you'll find a frog in your pocket." Stacy was a little horrified, but mostly just touched.

Alice handed her a tissue and helped clean off the jelly. "I keep my white blouses under lock and key," she said. "I never put one on until all the kids are safely asleep." She stood up. "Let's go see if Mom needs help."

Stacy followed Alice into the crowded kitchen with her arms folded over her chest, afraid that someone would notice the stain on her blouse. But people only smiled and said hello—except for one cousin, who remarked rather loudly that Pete certainly had good taste in girls—and after a few minutes, Stacy relaxed. She looked around for something to do and joined Pete's sister Margaret, who was peeling potatoes at the sink.

"Pete told us that you make mugs and things," Margaret said. "He said they're really pretty."

"It's nice of him to say so," Stacy replied, pleased. She'd never peeled a potato before, but it wasn't all that hard, although Margaret was twice as fast.

"If I got some clay, would you show me how to do it?" Margaret asked.

"We could do some hand-building, maybe," Stacy said, slicing her thumb. "If we had room enough."

"Oh, we've got room," Margaret said enthusiastically. "We could do it on the kitchen table."

Stacy sucked her bleeding thumb. "Won't your mother object?"

Margaret stared at her. "Why? Dad and Pete build their model airplanes there, and the twins fingerpaint there. I'm sure it'd be okay."

Stacy shook her head. She couldn't imagine *her* mother letting her work with clay in the kitchen. But then, Sydney's kitchen was entirely different, with its carefully orchestrated decor and high-tech gadgetry. She looked around at the bowls of salad and heaps of cauliflower and squash. Had she ever seen her mother cooking *real* food in her kitchen? One thing was certain: Sydney had never peeled a potato before.

Pete's mother, a calm, matronly woman with sandy hair, came up behind them and handed Stacy the baby. "I've got to do something about the rolls, Stacy," she said. "Would you mind washing the baby's face? The washcloths are in the bathroom, in the hall." She put the baby into Stacy's arms, glancing at her bleeding thumb. "Did you hurt yourself?" she asked with concern. "Get a Band-Aid while you're in the bathroom."

Holding the baby, Stacy looked around nervously. She'd never really held a baby before, and she wasn't sure she was doing it right. But Margaret had gone off to fix squash, and Alice had disappeared, so she located the bathroom herself, found the washcloths, and began to wash the baby's face. The baby began to howl.

"I know *exactly* how you feel," Stacy said grimly, still scrubbing. "You like yourself just the way you are." The baby stopped howling and stared at her, eyes like saucers. "Still," Stacy added, "you *do* look much prettier with a clean face." Still holding the baby, she began to look for the Band-Aids.

The baby began to chuckle and grabbed at Stacy's pearl necklace.

"I've been looking for you," said the painted Indian, coming into the bathroom. "I want to show you my fort."

"I've been washing the baby's face," Stacy explained.

The baby chortled and pulled at Stacy's necklace again. The string snapped, and pearls scattered all over the floor.

"Oh, no," Stacy moaned. Pearls everywhere. Some of them had already rolled down into a crack by the baseboard.

The Indian took the baby and put her into the empty bathtub. "How come you're so upset?" she asked, getting down on her knees. "Is it your favorite necklace?"

"Well, sort of," Stacy muttered. She found a paper cup on the sink and began to pick up pearls.

"Don't worry. When we've found them, I'll help you put them on another string. Good as new."

Alice opened the door. "What's going on?" she asked, looking at the baby in the bathtub and Stacy and the Indian on their hands and knees. "Why is the baby eating toothpaste?"

"La, la, la," the baby chanted gleefully, holding up a tube of toothpaste.

"The baby broke Stacy's pearls," the Indian told her.

"Par for the course." Alice sighed and got down on her knees beside Stacy. "I should have warned you," she said. "The other thing I keep locked up is my jewelry. The breakable stuff, anyway."

"You guys've been in there for a whole *hour*," one of the twins said urgently, out in the hall. "I have to go."

"We have to find *all* of Stacy's pearls," the Indian told him, sounding important. "Use the upstairs one."

"La!" said the baby with immense delight, squeezing the tube hard. A blob of toothpaste shot out of the tube and hit Stacy in the middle of the forehead. She tried to wipe it off, but it smeared.

"You look like an Indian, too," the girl said with a giggle. "You've got blood on your face, and toothpaste, too."

"I know, I know," Stacy said. Jelly on her blouse,

blood and toothpaste on her forehead—what would happen next in this crazy family?

Alice found her a Band-Aid. "Stacy," she said with a grin, "has anybody told you lately what a good sport you are?"

"A good sport?" Stacy asked. In her whole life, nobody had ever said that she was a good sport. "Well, thanks for the compliment."

"Listen, I have to go *here*," the twin said plaintively. "Somebody's locked a dog in the upstairs bathroom, and I'm afraid of dogs."

"Go ask Margaret to let the dog out," Alice said through the door. "Her boyfriend put it there to keep it from chasing the cat."

Pete stuck his head into the bathroom. "Alice, Mom wants you to mash the potatoes," he reported. He looked at Stacy. "What are you doing on the floor?" he asked, puzzled. "How'd you get grape jelly on your blouse? And what's that on your face?"

For a minute Stacy panicked: she knew she looked like a wreck, crawling around on the bathroom floor in a stained blouse with a glob of bloody toothpaste stuck to her forehead. "Well, I . . ." she began. "I mean, it's a long story. That is . . ." She sat back on her heels and looked at him helplessly, beginning to giggle. And in a minute they were *all* laughing. Stacy, Alice, Pete, the Indian—even the baby was smiling.

Pete shook his head, his eyes warm. "I just knew if I left you alone with this crazy bunch for very long,"

he said, "you'd never be the same again, Stacy
Swanson."

Dinner was served at two tables, one in the dining
room and the other in the living room. Stacy, sitting
next to Pete, decided that there were about twelve
people at their table—she couldn't be sure because a
couple of kids kept disappearing under the table,
where she suspected they were feeding the cat. They
were all crowded shoulder to shoulder, but everybody seemed to think that was the way Thanksgiving
was *supposed* to be, and the babble of conversation
grew louder by the minute.

"What do you think?" Margaret asked, next to
her.

"I think it's—amazing," Stacy said, hoping that
was the right word. "It's very different from what I'm
used to at home," she added. Last Thanksgiving, her
mother had given a small party, catered by one of
Boston's best restaurants. The dinner—*nouvelle cui-
sine*—had consisted of a clear soup, a slice of veal
with mushroom sauce, and a pear poached in wine.
There'd been restrained conversation, punctuated by
the clink of silver and crystal against a muted background of classical music. In comparison, today's
dinner was like a village harvest celebration. The
only thing was, she was having more fun today than
she'd had with Sydney. Everyone here was so relaxed.

Pete's father stood up, picked up the glass of milk

on the table in front of him, and raised it in a toast. Both tables fell silent.

"Here we all are, together again," he said, "family and old friends and"—he smiled at Stacy—"some special new ones. On this Thanksgiving, let's all be thankful for one another." There was a happy chorus of agreement, and everybody raised their glasses.

On the other side of Margaret, Alice reached over to clink her glass against Stacy's, Pete's, and Margaret's. "Hey, to new friends," she toasted with a warm smile.

Pete nudged Stacy. "Pass your plate."

When her plate came back, it was loaded. Stacy leaned in close to Pete and whispered, "But I can't possibly eat—"

"So how do you like Hawthorne?" asked one of the cousins, leaning forward across the table.

Next to her, another cousin chimed in, "Pete tells us that you've traveled all over Europe. Where have you been? What's it like compared to here?"

After answering the questions about Hawthorne and telling the cousins about Europe as quickly as she could, Stacy dug in: turkey, stuffing, cranberry sauce, mashed potatoes, and giblet gravy. While she and Alice and Margaret debated the pros and cons of joining a sorority in college, she finished off sweet potatoes, creamed onions, and cauliflower. Then, while Pete and Margaret argued about whether the high school should have a football team, she ate the huge slice of pumpkin pie that had appeared in front of her.

"I thought," Pete remarked, looking at her plate, "that you couldn't possibly eat all that."

"I'm full of secrets," Stacy said, sitting back. Actually, she'd been surprised by her healthy appetite. Suddenly she felt a pair of arms around her neck.

"Don't worry," the tomboy Indian said, "I washed my hands. I just wanted to measure your neck so I can fix your beads—pearls, I mean. Be right back!" She scampered away as Stacy sat in astonishment. So this was what life was like in a big family.

Margaret poked her. "Hey, I hope you don't mind helping with the dishes," she said, pushing her chair back. "Even guests have to wash dishes in this house."

There was no dishwasher in the big, old-fashioned kitchen, but the Youngs sure could have used one, Stacy thought. Especially today—there was a mountain of plates and silver. Stacy found a dish towel and began to help.

"How's your thumb?" asked Mrs. Young, coming up to her. Stacy showed her the Band-Aid, and Mrs. Young patted her shoulder. "Wounded in the line of duty," she said. "That'll get you a gold star."

She went to the refrigerator and examined a sheet of paper studded with gold stars that was taped to the door. She added Stacy's name at the bottom and pasted a star beside it. "There," she said, smiling. "I know it's a kid's game," she whispered, "but it gives the little ones something to live up to when they know that *everybody* gets stars around here."

Stacy stared at her name and then at Mrs. Young.

This was the nicest family she'd ever met. "I haven't had a gold star since I was seven," she said.

"Well, then," Pete's mother said briskly, "you were long overdue, weren't you?"

After the kitchen clean-up, she and Pete played Trivial Pursuit with a group of cousins, and soon it was time to go. Stacy got a hug from Pete's mother and a handshake from his father. Alice and Margaret followed them to the door.

"It was fun," Margaret said. "Please come back."

"We're not just saying that, either," said Alice. "We mean it. But next time, wear your grubbies. The twins never run out of grape jelly." Stacy laughed as she hugged Alice good-bye, and she kept on laughing as she and Pete ran through the falling snow and climbed into the pickup.

When they got to Rogers, Pete parked the truck and walked Stacy to the stairs. "Thanks," she said a little shyly. "It was a wonderful day." But somehow, the words didn't quite measure up to the way she was feeling inside. She thought of her gold star on the refrigerator door. Pete—and his family—had accepted her without question. She hadn't had to worry about how she looked or what she said—they just liked *her*. It made her feel wonderful.

Pete squinted up at Rogers. Stacy had left the lamp on in the living room, and suite 2C's window was the only lighted one in the whole dorm. "Hey, you know, you're going to be lonesome up there tomorrow, all by yourself."

Stacy frowned. She didn't want to think about

tomorrow while she was still wrapped in the warmth of the afternoon. "Ugh, tomorrow," she said. "Tomorrow I've got to get serious about finding a home for Bandit, and I've got to study, and—"

"Bandit?" asked Pete. "You mean your kitty?"

Stacy nodded and told him about Bandit's victory over the mouse and about Pam's eviction notice. "He has to be gone by the end of the holiday," she said. Suddenly she looked at Pete. "You know, I wonder..." she began.

"Hey, I've got this great idea..." Pete said at the same time, and then they both laughed.

"Do you suppose your mother would *mind* having another cat?" Stacy asked tentatively.

Pete shook his head. "What's one cat more or less?"

"You're not kidding?" Stacy asked. If Bandit went to live at Pete's house, she could see him sometimes.

"Hey, would I kid about such a serious matter?" he asked. "Sure, we'll take Bandit." He looked up at the dark sky, the snowflakes sifting down. "Actually, what I had in mind, if this snow keeps up, was taking the sled to Patrick's Hill tomorrow. Will you go with me?"

Stacy looked up at him. The snowflakes glistened on his curly hair, and his eyes sparkled in the darkness of the night. This time, Stacy told herself, she wasn't going to make the same mistake. "Yes," she said. "Going sledding sounds good."

"Okay." For a minute he didn't move. Then he

bent forward and kissed her cheek. "Happy Thanksgiving, Stacy Swanson," he said, turning to go.

"Pete?" Stacy called after him. "Thanks for today and, well, everything. You know."

"Yeah. I know." He got into the truck and waved good-bye.

Chapter 16

Pete came by the next day at around two o'clock with an old wooden sled in the back of the truck. Stacy, wearing her blue jacket and mittens, ran out to meet him, and they drove to the top of Patrick's Hill. The snow was already beginning to melt in the afternoon sunshine, but they sledded down a dozen times, taking turns pulling the sled back up. On their last slide, they got into a rough-and-tumble snowball fight that ended with Stacy, giggling wildly, shoving a handful of snow down the back of Pete's jacket and getting her face rubbed with snow in return.

"Oh, stop," she begged, laughing so hard she couldn't sit up. Her hood had fallen back, and her hair was matted. She spit out a mouthful of snow.

"Uncle," Pete demanded, threatening her with another handful of snow. "You've got to say uncle."

"Oh, uncle," Stacy gasped, giving up and lying flat on her back in the snow. "Uncle, uncle, uncle."

Pete helped her sit up. "You okay?" he asked, brushing the snow off her face. "I didn't hurt you, did I?"

"No." Stacy laughed and pushed the wet hair out of her eyes, "except that I'm a complete mess."

Pete looked at her. He took off his glove and wiped a snowflake from her mouth. "Did anybody ever tell you that you're beautiful even when you're a mess? With snow all over you, or toothpaste, even?"

Stacy shook her head, for a minute looking away from the intensity of his gaze. "No," she said softly, "nobody ever said that to me before." Then she looked at him again, and her heart skipped a beat. She knew he was going to kiss her, and as he pulled her into his arms, she let herself lean against him.

"Uncle," she whispered again, and closed her eyes as she felt his lips on hers.

On Saturday night, Stacy put Bandit in a box to take to Pete's house in her Mercedes. "Are you sure it's okay?" she asked Mrs. Young anxiously when she arrived. "He's a very good cat, and he catches mice. But I don't want to impose. . . ."

"It's no imposition." Mrs. Young laughed as they watched the twins carry Bandit off to meet the other cat. "The kids will love him. And of course you can borrow him any time you like."

"Borrow him?" Stacy said. "What a wonderful idea!"

"Sure," Pete told her. "Whenever the mice get out

of hand in Rogers, all you have to do is put Bandit on duty for a day or two. I'm sure he'd lick the problem."

"Ha ha," Stacy laughed sarcastically. "Stick to engineering, not comedy."

Later, they drove to a club on Patterson Road to dance. "I'm a liberated guy," Pete said with a laugh as they got into Stacy's car. "I don't mind riding with a liberated woman in her Mercedes—especially when she's buying the gas."

"I'm just worried about one thing," Stacy said as the Mercedes purred into action.

"Yeah, what's that?" Pete asked, playing with the push-button windows.

Stacy grinned and pointed toward Pete's pickup, parked in the driveway. "I'm afraid your truck will get jealous."

With a laugh, he reached over to tousle her hair.

At the club, Stacy discovered to her pleasure that Pete was a terrific dancer. She didn't need to worry about anything—she just followed his lead and gave herself up to the beat of the music.

"Hey, don't look now," Pete murmured against her hair as they danced a slow dance, "but isn't that Brenda at that table? I *think* that's the girl Roni pointed out to me at the game."

"Brenda!" Stacy exclaimed. "What's *she* doing here? Why didn't she go back to Texas for Thanksgiving?" She closed her eyes. It had been such a great holiday, but seeing Brenda made her think of everything she still had to deal with—the rumors, the

sorority, her unfinished schoolwork, her professors
. . . the list was too long.

Pete shrugged. "How should I know? Why don't
you ask her?"

"Ask her? After what she tried to do to me?"
Stacy laughed shortly. "You've got to be kidding.
Why should I even stoop to *talk* to her?" They
danced silently for a minute, then Stacy said, "In
fact, if you don't mind, I'd like to leave."

"But I *do* mind," Pete said, holding her off and
looking at her. "You're too strong to be chased off the
dance floor by a loser like Brenda."

Stacy buried her face in his shoulder. "But every
time I think of what everybody's saying about
me . . ."

Pete shook his head. "By the time everybody gets
back from Christmas break, the whole thing will be
forgotten. Alex will have found something else to
make him feel like the Big Man on Campus, and
everybody will understand that the whole thing was
pure rumor. That's one thing about a college
campus," he added. "Rumors come and rumors go
—they don't hang around forever."

They danced in silence while Stacy thought about
what Pete had said, about everything that had happened in the last few days, and about the changes
that seemed to be happening inside her. Was she
strong enough to confront Brenda? Maybe she
wasn't giving herself enough credit.

"Well, maybe you're right," she muttered. "Let's
go say hello."

"What did you say?" Pete asked, bending closer.

"I said 'uncle,'" Stacy replied. Laughing, they went over to Brenda's table. She was sitting with another girl, and they were deep in conversation.

"Hi, Brenda," Stacy said with the warmest smile she could muster.

Brenda looked up. "Why, Stacy!" she exclaimed uncomfortably, as if Stacy had overheard what she was just saying. "How *are* you? How's your ankle?"

"Oh, my ankle's *so* much better," Stacy said. "It's sweet of you to ask. Didn't you go home for the holiday?"

"No, I'm visiting my cousin Sandy," Brenda said, nodding at the other girl. Then she sneaked a glance at Pete. She obviously thought he was cute.

"Oh, let me introduce you to my friend," Stacy said smoothly, looping her arm through Pete's. "This is Pete Young. He lives in Hawthorne Springs," she added with measured emphasis.

"Listen, Stacy," Brenda said, "I want to tell you how sorry I am about the election. I think it was a rotten shame that—"

"As a matter of fact," Stacy said, interrupting, "the election was so close that the executive committee's decided to have an advisory board for the pledges. Nancy's asked me to be on it."

"An advisory board?" Brenda said.

Stacy put a hand on Brenda's shoulder and smiled sweetly again. "And I want to assure you, Brenda, that I don't have any hard feelings about what you did. None at all." Beside her, Pete was trying not to laugh. He squeezed her arm as if to say, I'm right here if you need me. But he could see that she didn't.

Brenda twisted in her chair. "Hard . . . feelings?"

Stacy nodded. "I'm sure you'd never *intentionally* damage anybody's reputation. And you couldn't *possibly* want to get a reputation as a gossip—that's so ugly and *juvenile*. That's why I'm sure that you made an honest mistake." She smiled sweetly at Brenda. "Isn't that right?"

Brenda stared at her, openmouthed. "Oh, absolutely right," she said. "It *was* just a mistake, Stacy," she lowered her eyes. "I hope you believe me."

"You were wonderful," Pete whispered into Stacy's ear as he danced her away from Brenda's table.

Stacy smiled. "You really think so?"

"Yeah. I mean, I don't want you to go getting a swelled head or anything, but I'd say that you're getting to be just about perfect."

"Just about?" Stacy teased.

"Well, aside from being too skinny." Pete laughed and ducked the swipe Stacy took at him. Then his arms tightened around her, and he kissed her on the neck. "Just about," he whispered.

By six o'clock on Sunday evening, Stacy had finally managed to get caught up with about half her homework—not all of it, the way she had hoped, but enough so that she could see some light at the end of the tunnel. It looked as if she were going to have to come to terms with getting a lousy grade in music appreciation. She'd spent so much time making up the quizzes that she was behind again. But at least she was making an effort, she reminded herself.

Suddenly Terry burst through the door with Sam

and Roni right behind. "Stacy! What's up?" asked Roni.

"Where's Bandit?" said Terry, looking around.

Sam smiled. "Don't tell me you've been sitting here studying *all* weekend, Stacy."

Stacy grinned. "Bandit's over at Pete's house," she said, "and no, I haven't studied all weekend."

"Pete?" Sam asked with a glance at Roni and Terry.

Terry opened the refrigerator. "You didn't eat your turkey bologna," she pointed out. "Or the cranberry sauce or the stuffing mix."

"I couldn't," Stacy said carelessly, stretching. "I was too stuffed with *real* turkey. And anyway, there wasn't time, what with going sledding and dancing and . . ." She laughed at the looks of astonishment on her suitemates' faces. "What's the matter? Did you think I'd just sit around the dorm and feel sorry for myself all weekend?"

Roni sat down on the sofa. "So tell," she ordered.

"Well," she began, "you remember that bell you gave me—the one that you're supposed to ring to summon your Prince Charming?" She grinned. "Well, I rang it and . . ."

Half an hour later, Stacy was finally winding up her story. "I don't know how things are going to turn out," she said a little more soberly. "I mean, I'm still a city person and Pete is a small-town guy, and I doubt if either of us will change enough to make it work over the long term. I still haven't resolved anything with my parents—in fact, I didn't even *hear* from them over the holiday. And I'm probably going to get a stupid D in music appreciation, because I'll never get caught up. But I think I'm sort of beginning to get a handle on things, anyway." She made a face. "The bad part is that I ate so much over the holiday I've gained two pounds. I guess I'll have to diet extra hard for the next week or two, and do some extra laps. I'm sure it'll come right off."

The girls exchanged glances. "Maybe this is a good time," Roni said, nudging Terry.

Terry looked at Sam. "I thought you were going to. . . ."

"No," Sam whispered. "We agreed that *you* would."

"Oh. Well, uh, Stacy," Terry said, squirming uncomfortably, "we were wondering if you've ever thought about the possibility that you might have . . . well, you know, a problem with food?" She paused. "I mean, we don't want to make you mad, but we've been thinking . . ." She looked helplessly at Sam.

"That is," Sam said, picking up where Terry left off, "we've been thinking that maybe you ought to see somebody, like a counselor or something. About . . . well, about eating disorders."

Stacy looked at them, feeling the old anger stir slowly within her, mixed with hurt and embarrassment. Then she remembered the conversation she'd overheard on the way to the Alpha Pi house, when one of the girls had said she was so skinny that she wasn't even pretty. And what Pete had said last night, about her being too skinny to be perfect.

"Is it true," she asked hesitantly, "that people think I'm too . . . well, *too* skinny?"

"Well," Terry said slowly, "I guess some of them do. I just wonder why you keep dieting when you don't have anything left to lose."

"Dr. Emerson gave me the name of somebody here on campus who's organized a group on eating disorders," she said slowly. "Maybe it would be a good idea for me to call her and find out when the meetings are. What do you think?"

Roni stared at her, startled. "Yeah, maybe," she said. "You mean you're not mad at us?"

Stacy sighed. "Yeah, I guess I *am* angry, in a way. But in another way I'm not, if that makes any sense. I'm finding out that it's really not a very good idea to get mad at your friends when they tell you the truth." She smiled. "If you can't trust your friends, who *can* you trust? . . . To coin a phrase."

Terry came over and put her hand on Stacy's forehead. "You sure you don't have a fever?" she asked with mock anxiety. "You're not acting like yourself."

"Well," Stacy said tentatively, "maybe that's because I've changed, or I'm changing—or something." She laughed. "I guess maybe I don't like the old Stacy a lot, when I look back at her. She must have been pretty rotten sometimes. How did you guys ever stand her?"

Roni screwed up her face. "Well, now," she said, pondering, "that's a very good question. There were some days when we thought about throwing her containers of yogurt over the balcony. . . ."

"Or changing the locks," Sam reflected.

"Or putting ice cubes in her bed," Terry said. "But

we could tell that there was a heart of gold under all those loose diamonds."

"And we hung in there to the end," Roni finished melodramatically.

"Yeah, but it's not over yet," Stacy cautioned. "I mean, I wouldn't want you guys to think I was getting to be *too* perfect."

"Too perfect?" Roni hooted. "Too perfect?"

Stacy ducked just in time to avoid the pillow that came hurtling toward her head.

"Hold still, Terry," Sam commanded as Terry squirmed in her chair to look at herself in the mirror. Stacy stopped doing her own makeup long enough to see what sort of transformation Sam and Roni had created for Terry. Not bad—she might even look pretty if she'd stop scowling.

"Really, Sam," Terry was saying, a frown wrinkling her forehead, "I don't think this is a very good idea." She glanced at the brand-new lacy white dress hanging on the closet door. At Stacy, Sam, and Roni's insistence, she had agreed to buy it for the winter formal she and Stacy had dates to that evening. "I mean, I *like* Brian. He's a nice guy and all that, but I don't really know that we ought to *date* one another. It might distract us from our studies."

"That might be a good thing," Sam said firmly, the hairbrush in her hand. "Stacy, what do you think of this?" She had finally brushed Terry's shoulder-length hair into a ponytail and fastened it with a silver bow.

Stacy stood back and eyed Terry critically. "I

think," she told Terry, "that you shouldn't wear your glasses."

"Not wear my glasses!" Terry exclaimed. "How am I supposed to see?"

"You don't have to *see* to dance," Roni pointed out.

"I do," said Terry. "I have to see my feet, anyway. I'm a lousy dancer. I never got any practice in high school." She looked up, her brown eyes anxious. "Listen, you guys," she said desperately, "I *really* don't want to do this. I don't know what to *do* on a date!"

"But Brian is a friend," Roni reminded her. "After all, you two have been seeing one another every day for the last few months. So what's so different about tonight? And anyway," she added, "Stacy will be there to help."

"I don't *know* what's different," Terry said. "But my stomach hurts." She stood up. "I think I'm going to be sick."

"No, you're *not* going to be sick," Sam said, and pushed her back down again. "Stacy, where's your makeup?"

Stacy opened the drawer. "Help yourself," she said, going to the closet. "I'm feeling Christmasy— do you think I ought to wear a red dress or a green one?"

"Everybody else will be wearing red or green," Roni said. "It's the holiday. So be different—wear your black dress."

Stacy blushed. "Pete doesn't like my black dress,"

she said. "He says it makes me look . . . well, too skinny."

"Then wear the white one," Sam suggested. "The one with the V-neck and the full skirt." She was fishing in the drawer. "Don't you have any just plain old *brown* eye shadow, Stacy? I think brown would be good for Terry, don't you, with her brown eyes?"

Roni looked into the drawer. "Here's some glittery green stuff," she said. "That might be interesting."

Terry groaned. "Can't we just stick with the brown?" she asked plaintively. "I don't *want* to glitter."

Stacy took the white dress out of the closet. "Hey, Sam, isn't this the same dress I loaned you to wear to Dean Peters's party at the beginning of the semester?"

"Yeah, that's the one," Sam said. "Think of everything that's happened since then!" She shook her head. "I can't believe how much things have changed in just a few months."

Impulsively, Stacy leaned over and hugged Sam, then found her arms around Terry and Roni, too. "Just *think*," she said wonderingly. "Heaven only knows what's going to happen to us next semester!"

"Yeah," Terry echoed, gazing skeptically at herself in the mirror. "Heaven only knows." She shifted uncomfortably. "Listen, do you suppose we could have a little rehearsal before we go?"

"Rehearsal?" Roni asked, raising one eyebrow.

"Like a dance rehearsal," said Terry. "I mean, I haven't danced since ninth grade, and I know I'm going to get all my feet mixed up and . . ."

Terry stared at the others as they collapsed, giggling. "I fail to see," she said stiffly, "that there's anything *humorous* about this at all. I'm going to be humiliated, and all you can do is laugh." She looked at herself in the full-length mirror and assumed a dancing pose. Then she started laughing, too. "Please don't make me go!"

"It's okay, Terry," Stacy said, wiping her eyes. "I'll dance just behind you and give you instructions so you don't get mixed up. One-two-three, one-two-three."

Terry turned to her. "You'll be sure to stick close," she said, "just in case I get into trouble?"

Stacy smiled. "Yeah, I'll stick close," she said. And she meant it.

Here's a sneak preview of *Major Changes*, book number three in the continuing ROOMMATES series

"Great! You got reassigned to the theater for another semester," Rob Goodman said, walking into the backstage supply room.

Terry looked up from the inventory list she was checking against a trunk full of costume accessories. "Yes." She smiled, pleased. "My work-study adviser said somebody here requested me back."

Rob grinned. "Yeah, well, the director and I had a talk about it and we decided we liked the way you worked. Unfortunately, a lot of the other work-study students we get here aren't really interested in *working*. They want this assignment because they think there's something glamorous about the theater. Then they get caught up in the illusion of it and forget that there's a lot of work involved with *creating* that illusion."

Terry picked up a peach-colored straw hat with a

veil and a huge mass of flowers piled on the crown. "Well," she said, examining the hat for signs of damage, "it's not the illusion by itself that interests me." Absently, she put the hat on her head and began to search the list, looking for the item number. She found it and checked it off.

Rob sat down on another trunk. "You're not into fantasy and illusion?"

Terry picked up another, smaller hat. "A little fantasy once in a while doesn't hurt," she said, "as long as you don't get lost in it."

"And what about illusions? Don't you have any?"

Terry shook her head. "I'm a practical person. I like knowing exactly how things are." She put the hat back into the trunk.

"Then what is it that you like about the theater? Are you interested in acting?"

"No," Terry said firmly. "Definitely not. I would never want to be on stage, with everyone watching me." She thought for a minute. "I guess what I like is being around and seeing how everything goes together to *create* the illusion. I've always liked getting a behind-the-scenes look."

"Oh, so you've done theater before you came to Hawthorne, then," Rob replied.

Terry picked up a lacy shawl and inspected it. "A little—not as much as I wanted, because I had a job. But I worked on a stage crew one semester. I like the backstage stuff—watching the stage designers build the sets, and the costume and makeup people dress up the characters, and the actors create the characters. It always seems like a magician's trick to me. We begin with a bare stage and in just a few weeks—abracadabra—we've got a complete play." She threw the shawl over her shoulder and bent to look into the trunk. She hadn't meant to run on about herself like that, but he had seemed interested.

Rob regarded her thoughtfully. "You know, you look terrific in that hat," he said. "You've got exactly the right shoulders and neck."

Terry's head jerked up and the hat fell off. "Oh," she said. She could feel herself blushing.

Rob picked up the hat and turned it in his hands. "We're doing *My Fair Lady* this semester," he said thoughtfully. "You know, Eliza Doolittle doesn't have any illusions, either."

Terry nodded. "I *like* Eliza," she said. "She's got a lot of courage, going up against everybody's expectations and still managing to . . ."

The door opened. "Hey, Rob, the director wants you out front," a boy said. "Pronto."

Rob stood up and grinned. "That's the second time that's happened to you," he said. "Why don't we finish this conversation later, when there aren't so many interruptions. How about a Coke at the Eatery—around five, maybe?"

For a minute, Terry stared at him, not believing what she'd just heard. Rob Goodman was asking *her* for a date? Just her luck—it was the one day she already had plans.

"I'm sorry," she said. "I wish I could, but I've got to meet somebody at the library at five."

"Your boyfriend?" His question was casual, but not innocent. Terry's heart beat faster.

"No," she said. "Just a friend. Somebody I'm tutoring." She cleared her throat. "I could . . . I could meet you a little later," she ventured.

"Rats," he said. "I've got something to do later." Instantly Terry thought of the pretty blond girl she'd seen with Rob at the Honor Board initiation. "But maybe tomorrow. . ."

The door opened again. "Hey, Rob," the boy said, "Eric says to tell you if you don't come now, he'll come after you. With his lasso."

"Sorry," Rob said hastily. He put the hat on Terry's head, patted her on the shoulder, and then disappeared with a grin.

For a few seconds Terry sat without moving. Then, still wearing the hat and with the shawl over her shoulder, she got up and stood in front of the mirror that hung beside the door and stared at herself. She was still blushing.

It had drizzled off and on all afternoon, but the rain finally stopped when Terry got to the library. She made her way to the back of the second floor study area, where she and Brian had always worked last semester. He was already there at a table by the window, his head bent over a book.

"Hi, Brian," Terry said, sitting down across the table from him. "How's it going?"

"Hi," he said. "Let me make some room for you." He pushed the stack of books to one side. "Hey, I'm really glad we're doing this, Terry. I mean, I don't think I need a lot of help, but since you and I worked together so well last semester, it seems like a good idea. Don't you think so?"

Terry nodded, smiling a little at Brian's enthusiasm. "You're right, it is a good idea. Were you able to get copies of your finals from last semester?"

"No," Brian said, in a disgruntled tone. "Perkins said it was his policy never to give out old finals, and Matthews asked me if I was going to study them for this semester or whether I planned to sell them to the highest bidder in the dorm." He laughed a little. "So I guess we're going to have to do without them."

Terry sighed. "Well, I see their point. I'm sure there's a good market for used finals." She looked at Brian's biology book, lying open on the table in front of him. "Do you want to work on biology first? How about if I ask you some questions about the first chapter?"

Brian pushed the book toward her and stretched. "Well, if you want to know the truth, I'm ready for a break," he said with a yawn. "I've been reading this stuff for a couple of hours and I'm really sick of it. It's so boring sometimes. I guess I'm not feeling very motivated." He turned to Terry with a grin. "So how'd *your* day go?"

"You mean, since you woke me up at six A.M. and dragged me out into the rain?" Terry asked teasingly. "Well, I guess it wasn't so bad." She thought of her conversation with Rob Goodman. "Actually, it was a pretty good day, all in all. A couple of really nice things happened."

"Oh, yeah?" Brian asked. He leaned forward

with his elbows on his knees and peered at her curiously. "Like what kind of really nice things?"

"Well, I got my work-study assignment," Terry said,
"and I'm working in the Theater Department again this
semester. In fact, they liked my work so much last
semester that they asked me to come back." She leaned
back in her chair and looked out the window at the lake,
which was beginning to fade into the gray twilight. A
boy and a girl were walking on the bridge, hand in hand.
"It's nice to know that somebody appreciates you."

"Yeah, that's great," Brian said with a sigh. "So
what else? I mean, you said a *couple* of nice things
happened."

"Oh. Well, I don't know," Terry said, feeling a
little funny. The other nice thing was her conversation
with Rob, but she didn't really want to tell Brian
about it. "Um, I just talked to somebody who's kind
of nice, that's all."

Brian grinned and sat back, folding his arms. He
looked pleased. "Yeah? Well, I enjoyed talking to
you this morning a lot, too. I'm glad we decided to
get together this evening."

Terry cleared her throat nervously. She hadn't
meant *him*! She hoped Brian wasn't getting the
wrong idea about them. But maybe her roommates
were right—maybe he did want more from her than
friendship. But how could she tell him she wasn't
interested in him that way? She was only trying to
help him out, not make him fall in love with her.
What had she gotten herself into?